The House on

Hayden Pond

JESSICA MONKS

Dedicated to my son Hayden.

I love you to my moon.

Chapter One

The Beginning of the End

Sheriff Jon Bolton eased his cruiser up the long steep driveway to the white house at the edge of Hayden Pond. He had been to the Hollick place once before, when the original owners had reported a possible break-in. Nearing the top of the driveway, he pulled over a short distance from his deputies' car, which was parked, dark and unattended, near the front door. The moon was full and bright, with no clouds to hinder its silvery light.

Jon had sent his deputies — his own son, Thomas, with another young officer named Brian — to alert Roman Hollick, the home's new owner, that a child was missing. The young daughter of Bob and Ellen Stuart had been gone for almost two hours. Jon had a bad feeling the incident was something serious. While most missing children in Sheffield were kids who'd gotten lost playing in the woods or had wandered off to the local grocery store, this somehow seemed *different.* More *alarming.*

Jon had been so busy organizing and calling the search party members he hadn't noticed Brian and Thomas hadn't recently checked in.

As he sat in his idling cruiser, Jon picked up his radio. "Denise, would you call Henry Parker and put him through?"

The radio let out a quick burst of white noise as Jon waited for her response.

"Henry's on the line," replied Denise. "I've contacted the Westchester Police Department. They're on alert."

"Thank you, Denise. Start calling the other towns that border everyone you called. We need to get this under control quickly."

"Sure thing," responded Denise. "I'm on it."

"Henry, you there?" asked Jon.

"Yeah, what's going on?" replied Henry.

"The Stuarts' daughter, Molly, has gone missing. There were footprints outside her bedroom window—large footprints that trailed off into the woods."

"Let me get Sebastian and I'll head over there as quick as I can," said Henry.

"I'm up here at the Hollick residence,"
continued Jon. "Going to check on the boys. They
haven't checked in for a while…and Henry, I don't
feel good about this at all."

"We'll find her, Jon," said Henry.

Jon hung up his radio and sat in the car for a
moment. This case was the first time he felt the
situation was more than his department could
handle. The details raced over and over again in
his mind. He reviewed his case notes, making sure
to think through every detail. Ellen Stuart had put
her daughter Molly to bed at 8:15 pm. She then
went to check on her eight-month-old baby,
Glenn. About fifteen minutes later, she returned to
make sure Molly was asleep. The child had
vanished. The window next to the bed was open.

Outside the window, muddy tracks from a pair of large boots crossed the back yard before disappearing into the dense leaves at the edge of the woods.

The father, Bob Stuart, was out of town. He had been notified and was flying home.

The info had gone out to all the deputies: Molly Stuart—ten years old, medium height, last seen wearing a long white nightgown—presumed abducted by a mysterious intruder who had brazenly broken in through her bedroom window as she slept.

Focused on finding her, Jon had over twenty people en route to the Stuarts' house. Henry's prize bloodhound Sebastian had been trained in tracking. He would be their best asset.

Jon believed it was his duty as sheriff to know as much as possible about the residents of Sheffield. Jon had been to nearly every house at least once, and he took comfort in knowing almost every person who called the town home. The house on Hayden Pond, where he was now, had been sold to a man by the name of Roman Hollick. *He must be a very private sort of fella*, thought Jon. It had been over a year since Hollick had moved to Sheffield, and Jon had not yet had the pleasure of meeting him.

With a feeling of irritation, Jon thought that while his deputies had only been on the force for a year, there was no excuse not to check in with dispatch. Enforcing protocol was important to Jon, and always setting a good example was what made a good sheriff. Jon lived by the rules.

Those boys probably got to talking and lost track of

time. His optimistic thoughts always brought him

comfort.

Getting out of his car, he walked towards his

deputies' cruiser. *Strange they would leave it*

unattended. The cold air gave him goose bumps

and he could see his breath. Early fall had brought

a chill to the air. *Almost time for jackets*, he thought.

From inside the house came a dull light

glowing eerily in the cold moonlight.

He stopped. Something caught his eye. It

moved in the darkness — a shape scraping against

the ground. Pulling his flashlight from the holster

on his belt, he flashed its bright beam on the

driveway. First confused by what he saw, pausing,

he popped the button off his holster and placed a hand on his gun. It looked like legs sticking out from underneath the front of his deputy's cruiser. He started running, suddenly recognizing the familiar blue uniform pressed and neat with the sturdy black shoes. As Jon breathed deeply the cold fall air seemed to freeze in his throat. His panic increased with every step. As he drew nearer he could see that the pants were stained red and soaked in blood. The red pool branched out, creating small rivers on the pavement.

As Jon came around to the front of the cruiser Brian, his youngest deputy, was holding his neck. Jon dropped down to his knees next to him. *Not here not in my town! These things don't ever happen here! Can't be real!* His mind raced, trying to make sense of what he was seeing.

With every heartbeat the gaping wound on Brian's neck gushed.

Jon pulled his radio and called dispatch. "I have an officer down. Three Hayden Pond Road. Need immediate medical attention and backup to location." He looked around to make sure the area was secure. Knowing the nearest hospital was twenty-five minutes away, his mind flooded with worry. The words seemed to flow steadily until he reached the end and began to choke. "Please advise time to location," said Jon, almost afraid to ask. The young deputy's eyes screamed with the story of what had happened but he was choking and couldn't manage the words.

"Shh, it's ok," said Jon. "Hold on son, try not to talk."

Brian started slipping into shock. Jon held pressure on the wound to stop the bleeding. The blood felt warm running over his hands. It was all he could do until help arrived. The memories Jon held of Brian's life came rushing back. Brian was like a son to him, and best friends with his own boy since kindergarten. With no father around, Jon had basically raised him. Jon was the reason Brian had gone to the police academy and joined the Sheffield Police Department. Brian's eyes were unfocused and his body twitched with every last effort to survive.

Then there was nothing a blank stare.

He was gone.

"Sheriff, this is dispatch," crackled the radio. "Eighteen minutes to location. Backup and ambulance en route."

Jon's eyes filled with rage. He knew there was nothing he could do — the boy was gone. Then a rush of reality came over him. He remembered they were patrolling together that night, and whispered "Thomas." Picking up his gun, he turned to the house and rose to his feet. Stopping for a brief second to click the safety off his weapon, he prepared himself for what lay ahead. He moved up the steps to the front door, barely making a sound. Pushing aside all procedures and protocols, ignoring his training and teachings, he was not waiting for backup this time. He kicked open the front door with such force it slammed against the wall with a loud bang. The love for his boy pushed him to abandon the rules. His heart filled with an aching pain and time seemed to freeze.

There in front of him was Thomas, hanging by a rope around his neck attached to the top banister of the second floor. Across his legs just under the knee was a deep laceration. The house was silent. All Jon could hear was the creaking wood supporting the slightly shifting weight of the rope and noise of the dripping blood hitting the wooden boards like a heartbeat bump bump… bump bump… bump bump. Aiming high at the banister, he breathed deep. Focusing intently, he squeezed the trigger four times. The banister shattered and Thomas's lifeless body fell into Jon's arms. He pulled the rope off, saying his name over and over again—"Thomas... Thomas, it's Dad... Thomas, I'm here now... Thomas?"

Lowering his son's limp body to the floor, he performed CPR, knowing in the back of his mind it held little hope. He had to try! There could be a chance—he *had* to try. He *had* to save him. How could he live without his son—his boy—his beloved Thomas?

For six long minutes he tried to revive him. Nothing—not a gasp, no movement, no heartbeat. He held his boy, hugging him tightly. How could this be real? How could this happen? Thomas had only graduated from the academy twelve months ago, and now he was gone. Jon hugged his son's body, tightly rocking him back and forth. It didn't matter how old Thomas was, that was his baby boy. He sobbed with devastation.

Barely having a moment to grieve Jon heard a scream. Loud and piercing, echoing through the kitchen from the basement, came the blood-curdling cry of a girl, distinctly a child — "*Help me!*"

Jon gently placed his son's body on the floor. Caressing Thomas's cheek, Jon nodded, acknowledging his loss. Then he picked up his gun from the pool of blood. His hand shook a little with the realization his gun was stained with his son's blood. Clenching his teeth and fists, rage again filled his body and took away every ounce of fear. He had lost so much! He must save her!

Moving with purpose and precision, he again refocused.

Walking through the dining room into the kitchen, he could see the basement door was open. Then he heard it again—the high-pitched shriek was not just a scream but a plea for life. Approaching the open basement door, his flashlight pierced the gloom. The bright beam revealed a light switch at the bottom of the stairs. He swiftly made his way down, walking with his flashlight over his gun, leading the way into the darkness. On both sides of the stairs the cement walls were damp and moldy, and stepping off the last rickety wooden tread he noticed the floor was mud. He leaned his back against the wall, sweeping his flashlight beam around the corners of a dark basement that stank like rotting, festering death. It made Jon breathe through his mouth — his nose could not stand the putrid stench.

The bright beam fell on a large pair of work boots. Raising his flashlight, he saw a large man drenched in blood sitting on the edge of what looked like a round well. Jon used his elbow to flick on the light switch. The light in front of him turned on first, then one after another seven more lights came to life, each delayed a few seconds. They made a sharp snapping noise as they lit and hummed loudly to stay illuminated. The lights revealed blood covering the man's face, hands, and clothes. He was a gleaming maroon mess with dark eyes and white teeth.

The man laughed slowly with a deep haunting voice that sent a cold shiver up Jon's back and raised the hairs on the back of his neck.

The man grinned sadistically, as if he were impressed with something he had done. "We have been waiting for you," he sneered. Sitting on the man's knee was a little girl. Jon recognized her immediately — she was little Molly Stuart. Blood streaked her long hair and tears trickled down her cheeks. The man's bloodstained hand covered her mouth while his other hand held a long sharp blade pressed against her throat. He smiled again, exposing those gleaming white teeth.

"He cried out for you," the man gloated.

The words stabbed Jon in the deepest part of his heart and echoed in his mind. Tears ran down his cheeks and his gun was shaking. In that moment, before Jon had his chance to negotiate his chance to save her, the man clenched his teeth and effortlessly cut through the little girl's neck.

Jon's face became a blank stare with shock. It was a deep hopeless wound; Molly's eyes became still as stone. The blood poured out onto her white nightgown like a red waterfall.

"No!" Jon yelled as the man threw her backwards into the well behind him. Jon gripped his gun tightly. "AAAAAHHHHHHHH," he screamed unloading the clip.

The man raised his hands, laughing loudly as the bullets hit their marks. He closed his eyes and fell backwards into the well.

Jon ran over to the well. It was about twenty feet deep. He could see the man's body floating in a deep pool of bloody water, with the demonic smile still pasted on his face. The sweat dripped off Jon's forehead, landing in the blood at the bottom of the well. The faint sound echoed back. The man's body slowly disappeared beneath the surface.

Jon could hear the sirens pulling down the road into the driveway and the deep bay of a hound nearing the house. He stared down into the well. It was like staring straight into hell.

Chapter Two

Thirty-Three Years Later

A battered blue work truck struggled up the long steep driveway to the old house with its grimy windows and broken shutters. Time had eaten away at its once-brilliant white paint, now covered in dirty mold. The only apparent life on the property consisted of the overgrown plants attempting to reclaim their land.

Two men stepped out of the truck. The deep blue eyes of Paul Bolton looked upon the old home with hope and promise. His cousin Ray walked toward the house, his hands held high. "Would you look at that!" said Ray. "Would you just look at it! Can you believe we never knew this place existed?"

Paul stared up at the house. He knew this could be something great. This could be his second chance. "Needs a lot of work, maybe a new roof," he said. "Nothing I wouldn't be able to handle."

They stepped carefully up the creaky stairs to the front door. Ray fumbled around with the keys. Paul grabbed the handle and pushed. "It's open," he said, smiling. They entered with wide-eyed wonder. As they walked into the house, the floorboards creaked with age.

"What's that smell?" said Paul covering his nose with his sleeve.

"The house has been shut up for a while. Probably just needs to be aired out," said Ray, trying to put a positive spin on his newfound inheritance. "I'll crack some windows. That should do the trick."

Paul stared up at the second floor banister. The wood was cracked and had protruding splinters. How strange that the banister had been damaged on that side of the railing, he thought.

Ray made his way through the dining room into the kitchen, opening up windows as he went along. The kitchen was full of light from the large window over the sink overlooking the back yard. There were three other doors leading from the kitchen — one each to the back yard, the garage, and the basement. He noticed the opened the pantry door hanging off its hinges. "It's got a nice size pantry for dry goods and what not," he said.

He moved over to the basement door. When he opened it he came face to face with a large spider web. Startled, out of spite he pulled down the web. Staring into the darkness he thought he heard a strange sound, like a whisper. Pausing for a moment he listened.

Ray's attention turned to Paul and he shut the door as Paul entered the room. The floorboard Paul stepped on creaked loudly.

"What did you say?" asked Paul.

"Ummm, oh, the pantry," answered Ray. "Take a look—it's full of space, nice and roomy, just needs a coat of paint."

Paul grasped the pantry door, wiggling it open. "You're right, it's going to need some paint and maybe some shelves. Sam's going to love it."

Opening the door leading to the garage to see his new work area, he was excited to see rows of shelving at the end of the garage and a workbench for his projects.

Ray started back towards the entryway. "Let's go upstairs and see if there's anything we can sell." Passing the dining room table, Ray picked up the checkerboard, sending the checkers across the table and onto the floor. "Kids probably use this place for a hangout," he said, tossing the board back onto the table. They walked up the stairs, both looking at the broken banister as they passed it. Paul ran his fingers over the splintered wood.

"Must have broken it while moving stuff out," said Ray.

Looking around upstairs, they found a bathroom and four bedrooms. "The girls can each have their own rooms," said Ray. "Even the baby can have his own room. Lots of space and windows. It's perfect for a growing family."

"How again did you just happen to get this house?" asked Paul shaking his head in disbelief.

"It wasn't in dad's will," replied Ray. "He must have forgotten all about it. The town found it in the deed listings and contacted me. We owed a couple thousand in taxes, but it was well worth it."

"I am truly in debt to you for this," said Paul. "I don't know what I would have done. Sam and the girls wouldn't have been happy living in a small city apartment. It would have broken their hearts having to give up our animals," he said, placing his hand on Ray's shoulder.

"We all fall on hard times," said Ray, looking around the room. "The lousy economy has touched everyone. You'll find some work, and in the mean time you got a hell of a project."

To Paul, the house was perfect in every way. It was even bigger than the house they lived in now and had more land. His mind raced with renovation possibilities. He had been laid off eight months earlier, and although he managed to keep afloat with odd jobs his savings had dried up and it was time for some hard decisions. All Paul wanted in this world was to make his family happy. He never realized his world could fall apart, and all it had taken was eight months.

They made their way back downstairs and outside. Walking over to the truck, Ray climbed in. Paul took one last look at his future home. He smiled and nodded—he had found hope. As they began the two-hour drive back to Paul's house, Ray, not being one to beat around the bush, dove right into business. "Okay, now here's the deal: you can move in right away—it will save you some money. You can have the house for two years rent free, but everything in the house needs to be painted, floors need to get refinished, ceilings painted, the whole shebang. After two years, we can sell the house and split the profit fifty-fifty, or you can buy me out for, let's say, one hundred thousand dollars. If you decide to keep it,

I'll even take it in monthly payments of a thousand dollars. What do you say?"

Nodding his head in agreement, a big smile appeared on Paul's face as he extended his hand. "You got yourself a deal," said Paul. Feeling like he was on cloud nine, he started to daydream of his happy family excited to see their new house. He hadn't felt like a hero in a very long time. Their lives were going to be different now. During the past eight months Paul had lost his job, his home, and his faith. He had been beaten down by bills. Now he could tell them with certainty that everything was going to be all right. It was bigger than any gift he could have imagined.

Chapter Three

The Move

A car filled with giggles of excitement and anticipation made its way up the driveway. The day had finally come — the big move! Sam glowed with excitement; she had waited two weeks and worked tirelessly to get the house packed. All the nights up packing 'til two in the morning were finally paying off. "Look at that girls... it's beautiful," said Sam, in awe of the enormous house. Paul smiled proudly, watching his gleaming wife dote over her new palace. "Girls, look — a pond," said Sam. "We can go swimming and fishing. There's plenty of room for a garden."

She peered through the windshield at the house. "Paul — is someone there?" she said.

"There shouldn't be… where?" replied Paul, looking at every window.

"Upstairs in the window — right there," said Sam, pointing to the upstairs bedroom.

"Ray had been up there and he opened all the windows to air out the house," replied Paul. "All I can see is the curtains blowing in the breeze."

"I thought I saw someone," said Sam.

"Well, I think the move has finally gotten to you," laughed Paul as Sam smiled and pushed his shoulder.

"Ha ha, very funny…very funny," said Sam.

Paul parked in front of the garage. "The pond borders the back yard and connects by a creek down in the woods to the pond across the street," he said, pointing out the sheer beauty of the property. He wanted to take a moment to appreciate the new house. The girls, however, had something different in mind. Being cooped up in the car for two hours and wondering about their new house had caused excitement that could no longer be contained. Bursting out of the car, they ran to the house, through the unlocked front door, and up the front stairs.

"I want to pick out my room!" said Emily, the oldest daughter, who had just turned eleven.

"Girls wait for me! I…," Sam tried to get out more than a few words while getting out of the car but gave up.

"It's all right, they're excited — let them go," said Paul.

Sam opened the back door of the car and unbuckled the baby seat. "Hi, sweet boy, did you have a good trip?" she said as she picked up her two-year-old baby boy Jack. Jack giggled with delight. Such a happy baby, it was rare for him to make a fuss about anything. After raising two girls, Sam was amazed at how well Jack handled life.

Sam could hear the excited footsteps of the girls racing upstairs. They had waited weeks to see the new house, and hearing all the wonderful things their dad had told them brought on feelings of adventure. After six years of sharing a room they were both ready for some much needed space.

Sam and Paul started walking towards the front door. Suddenly they heard a scream from the upstairs bedroom. Running into the house and up the stairs, Paul and Sam rushed with worry. "Girls...girls?" they both yelled.

Paul entered the first bedroom. The girls were standing over a dead raccoon, staring at it with amazement and disgust.

"Eww, that's so gross," said Emily.

"Daddy, what happened to him?" said Lily.

"I don't know, girls; maybe he was trapped in here without food or water," said Paul.

Sam walked over to the window looking out. "But Paul, the window's open. Why didn't he just leave?"

"I don't know," replied Paul. "Maybe something was wrong with him."

"Daddy, he stinks," said Lily, the middle child, who had just turned six years old.

"It's okay, girls — go downstairs while I clean up this mess," said Paul.

"I don't want this room," announced Emily. "It smells."

"This is our room, girls," said Paul. "You'll each have one of the smaller bedrooms."

"Come on girls, lots to unpack," said Sam, seeing the moving truck pulling into the driveway.

Sam went downstairs and outside to the car. She pulled a cat carrier out of the rear of the car and handed it to Lily. "Lily, here's Buttercream.

Take him upstairs for now and don't let him

out 'til we're finished unpacking."

Emily walked up to Lily and grabbed the cat

carrier. It was obvious Lily needed help carrying

the heavy box upstairs. Sam then opened the

larger crate that held the dog. "Hello, Kingston!

Did you have a good trip?" she said, running her

hands over his head and kissing his snout. A very

lazy Rottweiler, tired from his long journey,

stretched and yawned as he exited the crate. Sam

took him over to a tree and tied his long rope to a

branch. "You'll be better off here while we

unload," she said as she scratched his ears.

Paul walked over and looked into Sam's

beautiful hazel eyes. "This is going to be the start

of something big," he said.

Sam smiled as Paul pulled her in. "We *already* have something big — this is just icing on the cake," she said as Paul gave her a long kiss.

"Ewww!" the girls both yelled from the upstairs window in protest.

Their new house was going to be a fresh start and every member of the family felt hopeful.

Chapter Four

Meet Edgar

Early next morning, the house was busy with breakfast preparation. With so much that needed to be done, Sam had barely slept. The only sleep she had found was interrupted by a vivid nightmare that had kept her up the rest of the night. But being tired today wasn't an option — there was too much to do. She went over the day's plan with Paul. "I need to start unpacking the kitchen, then the bedrooms," she said, rubbing her face and letting out a yawn.

"Ok," replied Paul. "I'm going to fix the upstairs railing before someone gets hurt. It's not going to be pretty — I'm going to do a quick fix for safety so I can get started on the pantry. We can re-make the whole railing when I put in the new stairs."

After they had finished breakfast, Emily cleared the table. "Emily, can you watch Jack for me today so I can focus on the house?" said Sam.

"Sure," replied Emily. "Lily and I can take him outside for a while." Sam knew Emily would much rather watch Jack then unpack.

"Thank you sweetie, and let the unpacking begin!" said Sam, pouring another cup of coffee. Everyone went their separate ways.

It was a beautiful day. The girls were outside with Jack, and they were walking Kingston around the yard. "Lily, let's see where that path leads," said Emily. There was a dirt path that started a few steps into the woods. The

woods were thick on each side of the house and

the girls had plenty of room for exploration.

"Maybe we should ask Mom," said Lily.

"It's fine," replied her sister. "Mom just wants

us out of the house for a while and we won't go

far."

Emily picked up Jack and headed into the

woods with Lily and Kingston in tow. They

walked for about ten minutes before reaching the

creek. It was pretty, about fifteen feet wide, and it

ran through the woods and connected the two

ponds. Over the creek there was an old bridge

made of three logs that had been tied together.

Emily put Jack down. "Hold his hand," she said to

Lily in her big-sister voice.

"What are you going to do?" asked Lily, knowing her adventurous sibling.

Without responding, Emily jumped onto the bridge and started walking across.

"Emily, I don't think that's such a good idea," protested Lily. "Mom and dad would be mad if they saw you playing on the bridge."

"Mom and dad aren't going to find out, are they?" Emily said in a strict tone as she looked back at Lily. Kingston put his front paws on the end of the bridge and whined.

Emily suddenly jumped, startled by the creaking snap of branches behind her. She looked into the woods on the other side of the bridge. Kingston let out a few barks of disapproval. She thought she saw someone passing behind the trees. Frightened, she turned and ran back across the bridge, and then, picking up Jack, she started to run back to the house.

"Emily, wait up — I'm coming!" shouted Lily.

Sam was in the kitchen on her stepstool stocking the cupboards, while Paul was in the garage cutting up boards to fix the railing and make new shelves for the pantry. Life seemed in full swing again. Sam got down and walked around the dining room looking at her new home. Trying to take it all in, she still couldn't believe they had been so lucky. On the table in the dining room there was an old checkerboard. The checkers were all set up waiting for the next game. She picked up the old board, carefully sliding the checkers off. It was covered in dust and she blew it off, checking it over carefully, curious as to its story. Next to the board were a shot glass and an empty bottle of whisky. *Must have been an interesting game*, she thought, walking over to the drawers that were built into the wall. She pulled and pulled at the bottom drawer but it was stuck. "Paul's going to have his work cut out for him," she said, tugging a few more times trying to loosen it. Letting out a sigh, she stood up, pulled at the top drawer — which opened easily — and put the board inside. Picking up all the game pieces, she dropped them into the drawer on top of the board.

Her mind filled with ideas for the bottle and shot glass. She loved to reuse old things for decorating and her crafts. She carried the glass and bottle into the kitchen and placed them in the sink. *Time to start opening more boxes,* she thought. There were a couple of boxes without labels, which seemed like a good place to start. The first box revealed a few sets of Christmas lights. The second box had ornaments for the tree.

"Should I put these in the garage?" said Sam, holding up an ornament to show Paul.

"No, I really want to keep the garage for my restoration stuff and tools," replied Paul, knowing very well that once stuff started going into the garage it would fill quickly, and he didn't want to lose his planned workspace.

Sam nodded her head. "Ok, you're right — after all, we're going to need room in there for all my craft boxes," she laughed as Paul's eyebrows raised.

"Umm...," Paul said, trying to come up with a response that could save his garage from being overtaken.

"Don't worry, I'll stay out of the garage," said Sam playfully. Paul smiled in relief. "I wanted to make the dining room into a craft area anyway. You're just going to have to make me some shelves," she said as she walked away with the Christmas boxes.

Shaking his head, Paul watched her go into the dining room. "Now I'm making craft shelves," said Paul to himself, knowing very well he had just been deceived into another project.

"What?" called Sam from the other room. "I didn't hear you."

"Nothing," said Paul, biting his lip and trying not to laugh.

Sam made her way up the stairs. She paused at the top, looking around on the ceiling for an attic door. Not finding what she wanted, she searched through the rooms one by one. "How on earth am I supposed to get into the attic?" she whispered to herself. She opened the bathroom closet and put the box on the shelf. Stepping back, she spotted a hatch at the top of the closet. "There you are," she said, starting to climb up the shelves to reach the panel above her head. The panel was supported by four boards connected in a square. It felt cold, and it squeaked when she pushed it up. Dust drifted down from all sides. She gazed up into the opening. It was pitch black, with a musty smell from being shut up for so long and not well ventilated.

The panel tipped back, and from the darkness two eyes stared down at her.

"Aahhhhhhh!" Sam screamed and fell from the shelves onto the bathroom floor. The panel fell shut again. She covered her mouth and almost in tears when Paul came flying upstairs and around the corner.

"What happened? What is it?" said Paul, kneeling down to her.

She looked up to the ceiling of the closet and pointed to the attic panel. "There's someone in the attic! I *saw* him," she insisted.

Paul peered at the ceiling while he helped Sam to her feet. He gently pressed his hand to her stomach, signaling her to back up away from the closet. Leaning towards the wall, he grabbed the broom and slowly approached the closet. Listening for any movement, he raised the broom to the panel. Pushing the panel up until it flipped back and away, Sam again felt uneasy and grabbed the soap dish.

"If there's anyone up there, you better come out! I have a gun and I have no problem using it!" Paul said loudly with his intimidation voice. All Sam could hear was the kids outside playing in the yard. Paul looked over at Sam. "Are you sure you saw someone?" he said.

"I opened the panel and there were two eyes staring back at me and I lost my balance," replied Sam, annoyed at not being believed.

"Could it have been another raccoon?" said Paul.

"I'm pretty sure it was a person," she replied. "Go ahead — look for yourself."

Paul turned back to the closet and took a deep breath. He climbed the shelves up to the top and slowly peeked over the edge. Reaching up to a dangling cord, he pulled it and the light turned on. He saw a low unfinished space with a few chairs and some clothes covered with a thick layer of dust. He climbed up further until he was sitting on the edge of the hatch. He could feel the heat of the attic fighting with the cool air of the bathroom.

"Your right, Sam, there is someone up here,"

he called down through the hatch.

"Should I call the police?" said Sam ready to

run for the bedroom phone.

Paul tossed down what looked like a small

body. It landed at her feet. Sam knelt down and

picked up the old scarecrow dressed in farmer's

overalls. The face, with its glass eyes, had been

crudely stitched together. His material was

covered in soot and faded. Someone had taken the

time to stich real looking black hair sporadically

on its head

"You can call the cops, but I don't think he's

talking," said Paul, giggling at Sam.

"Creepy," said Sam as she sighed, shaking her head. She knew Paul was going to remind her about this for some time.

"Our uninvited guest has overstayed his welcome, and for this he shall be sent into exile," said Paul with a smile as he descended from the closet. "Come Edgar, to the garage with you." He was quite pleased that he had rescued his wife from the scarecrow.

"Edgar?" asked Sam.

"Yes, he reminds me of Edgar," said Paul lifting up the decrepit decoration.

"Ahh, the creepy gas station guy from home," said Sam.

"Yes—I shall call him Edgar," said Paul. As Paul started down the stairs with Edgar tucked under his arm, the girls were running into the house with Kingston.

"Cool—a scarecrow," said Emily.

"Yes, girls," said Paul. "Meet Edgar, who, after scaring your mother, will now reside in the garage." Paul went into the garage and sat Edgar up on the workbench. Stopping to take a good look at his newfound friend, he could barely stomach him. "You are hideous aren't you?," he said as he looked into the cold glass eyes of the old dirty scarecrow.

Paul went into the house and back to the kitchen.

The door to the basement was wide open. "Girls?" He heard a noise like something was moving about. "Kingston? Are you down there?

Come here, boy." He looked up through the kitchen window to see the girls in the back yard walking Kingston around toward the pond. "Hmm," he said heading down into the dark basement. The light switched at the bottom of the stairs snapped on loudly as eight dim light bulbs came on, leading him through the basement. The noise came again, this time like fingernails scraping on a blackboard. Paul walked through the basement past the boiler to a circular stone well covered with a thick round piece of wood. He put his ear down against the piece of wood, listening for the sound. It came again — a loud scraping that startled Paul and made him jump back and fall onto the cold dirt of the basement floor. He stood up, brushed his pants off, and listened again. "Probably just rats," he said to himself.

He jumped feeling two hands grab him from behind. He twisted to see Sam smiling at him.

"Looks like somebody else is awful jumpy," she said. "What's wrong?"

"Nothing, honey," replied Paul, fumbling around. "Just looking for a shovel."

"One day you'll be a better liar, but not today, Mr. Bolton, not today," Sam said as she walked up the basement stairs.

Chapter Five

Welcome to the Neighborhood

The next morning everyone met downstairs for family breakfast. A normally cheery Sam was moping around the kitchen.

"Everything ok?" asked Paul, taking a sip of his coffee. "You don't seem like yourself today."

"I had another nightmare last night that kept me up since three," replied Sam with a yawn.

"Oh really? What about?"

Sam sat down to the breakfast table. "Girls, don't forget to feed Buttercream." The girls jumped out of their seats and ran upstairs to feed their beloved cat. Sam started cutting up Jack's pancakes. She turned to Paul. "I dreamt I was walking through the house down to the

basement. The light would not work but for some

reason I didn't care. I *had* to go into the basement.

When I got downstairs, Jack was standing on the

edge of that old well wall, and as I ran towards

him, he fell into the well. I couldn't get to him in

time. I went to jump in but someone grabbed me

and held me back. He whispered, 'It's not real….

you can wake up now!' His voice was kind but I

could not stop wanting to get Jack. I struggled to

break away from him. All I could see were his

hands. He was wearing a very pretty gold ring. I

was so scared, and then everything turned cold. A

man started coming up out of the well. His face

was covered in blood and he began grabbing at

me and pulling the bottom of my nightgown.

Then I woke up. It was so real that I just couldn't go back to sleep. I even went and checked Jack but he was fast asleep."

Paul reached over and gently held her hand and kissed it. "It's ok. It's perfectly normal to have bad dreams. New house, it's a new neighborhood, a new town. Everything around us is new. You're bound to be nervous about moving your whole life."

Sam smiled and Paul moved his hand to her face, touching her lips. She tilted her cheek onto Paul's hand. "I know it's a silly dream," she said. "I'll sleep better tonight."

"I'm sure of it," replied Paul. "I have some work to do today. I'm going to the store for some shingles. I need to repair the roof before we get any leaks. Then I need to stop at Ray's house

and help him put up a fence. He's paying me to

help him."

"Ok," replied Sam. "I'll try to finish unpacking

the bedroom. Hopefully I can find the sheets."

Paul stood up and put his jacket on. Grabbing

the coffee pot off the counter, he filled Sam's cup

before kissing her on the head. "Have a good day.

I'll be back soon," he said.

Jack pulled at his jacket so Paul tickled him. "Be

a good boy and help mommy," laughed Paul as

Jack giggled.

"Of course he will, he's mommy's big helper,"

replied Sam, smiling at her delighted baby boy.

After Paul had left, Sam went upstairs to go

through some boxes of clothes. Folding each item

neatly into the drawers, she glanced out the window. While in deep thought about the design of her new garden, something caught her eye. She could have sworn that down in the back yard someone had walked briskly across her view. She walked over to the window and looked down and all over the yard, but saw nothing. With Paul gone, she was worried there was someone wandering around the house. Picking up Jack, she brought him into Emily's room. "Em, can you watch Jack for a minute?" she said.

"Sure," replied Emily as she picked up Jack and sat down with him on the floor in front of Lily.

Sam went downstairs, quickly moving through the rooms and looking out the front windows, but she saw nothing. Going through the dining room into the kitchen, she looked out the back

window over the sink. Standing up on her tiptoes

to get a better look, she leaned close to the glass.

Suddenly, an old woman appeared in the

window in front of her. Sam jumped back, holding

her chest.

"Shouldn't be here!" the old woman called out

before walking away from the window.

Sam ran to the back door and looked around,

but the woman was gone. Irritated by her

intruder, after locking the back door she hurried to

the front door. The old woman was now standing

in the driveway, looking up at the house.

"Excuse me, what are you doing here?"

demanded Sam, now in defense mode.

"You shouldn't be here," replied the old woman. "*No one* should be here. He promised no one would *ever* be here!"

"Well ma'am, I don't know who you talked to, but this is our home and we intend on being here for a long time."

"You'll be here longer than you want to be," replied the old woman. "*Much* longer."

Sam looked at her, perplexed at the strange exchange of words. Who was this unwelcome intruder?

A man came hurrying around the corner at the bottom of the driveway.

"Mom, what are you doing here?" said the man, looking first at the old lady and then at Sam as he jogged up the drive. "I am so, so sorry, miss," said the man as he approached the old lady and turned her around. "This is all my fault. I'm sorry. This won't happen again, I promise."

"It's ok, she didn't bother me," said Sam, realizing the old woman was not of sound mind.

"Sorry — where are my manners?" He took his hands off his mother's shoulders and approached Sam with his hand extended. "Hi, my name is Glenn Stuart. This is my mother Ellen. She has advanced Alzheimer's, which has gotten worse since my dad died a few years ago. I'm keeping her home as long as I can. She's usually really good, but I left her on the porch to make some tea and she went on an adventure."

"I'm Sam Bolton," offered Sam as she shook Glenn's hand. "I live here with my husband Paul and our three kids."

"Please to meet you. It's nice to have new neighbors. I don't remember anybody ever being in this house, even when I was a kid. I was never allowed over here. My mother forbade it."

"We've only been here since yesterday, but we plan on staying a long time," said Sam.

The girls appeared with Jack in the doorway behind her.

"Hi girls," said Glenn. "Pleased to meet you. I'm your new neighbor."

"Take those babies and *leave this place*," hissed Ellen.

"On that note, we best be going," said

Glenn. "Come on, mom, let's leave the nice people

alone." He turned to Sam. "I'm sure we'll see you

again soon if you need anything. We're the first

house on the right. It's just a little ways up."

Putting his arm around the old lady, he guided

her down the driveway.

"Come back for a visit sometime," said Sam.

"Paul would love to meet you, I'm sure."

Sam went into the house. "Come on girls, we

need to get some work done before daddy gets

home," she said as she closed the door and headed

upstairs.

"Who was that man?" asked Emily.

"That was our new neighbor, Glenn, and his

mother, Ellen. They seemed very nice." Sam was

relieved that her intruder was just old and confused. She used to be a nurse and had worked with Alzheimer's patients. What a good person Glenn must be to take care of his mother! Most people can't handle their aging parents, especially with the onset of Alzheimer's. It made her feel good that the neighbor seemed so kind and patient.

Chapter Six

The Trouble with the Girls

Sam went back upstairs to unpack her clothes while Jack busily played on the floor with his toys.

"Mom, I can't find Buttercream!" said Lily, sounding irritated.

"Honey, maybe he just doesn't want to be found right now. Maybe he has this big house to explore and he's busy investigating."

"I'm going to check downstairs for him," said Lily, determined to locate her cat.

"Ok, but tell your sister it's her turn to do dishes. The soap and sponge are in the garage."

"Ok," Lily replied, racing down the stairs to look around the dining room. "Buttercream, here boy, Buttercream, kitty kitty," called Lily. She crossed the entry way into the living room. "Emily, Mom said it's your turn to do the dishes, and the soap is in the garage."

"Ok, fine," replied Emily, sticking her tongue out at Lily, who returned the gesture. Emily sighed and tossed her book onto the coffee table. She went into the garage, looking around for soap. She found a box on the shelf, and a sponge. The light was on over the workbench. She walked over to it, and after looking around she turned off the light. *Someone must have been in the garage and left it on.* Lifting the headphones from around her neck she put them over her ears. Listening to music always made chores go by much faster.

She turned around as Buttercream dashed

through her legs and made her jump.

"Buttercream! You naughty cat! You almost

tripped me!" she said as she made her way

towards the door to the kitchen. She turned

around and saw the scarecrow sitting on the end

of the workbench. Funny, she hadn't noticed him

there before. The old scarecrow gave her an

uneasy feeling, like he was watching her. She

backed up the stairs into the kitchen, watching the

scarecrow, before shutting the door. Staring at him

through the window in the door, she turned the

lock. She paused for a moment to look at him—his

clothes old and dark, his little rubber boots stuffed

with straw. Who would make such a creepy

monstrosity? *That thing could scare away more than birds*, she thought.

With soap and sponge she went over and turned on the water. It was time for some music. She turned up her walkman and started to dance around, bobbing her head. Lily entered the kitchen but Emily did not notice her.

"Buttercream? Here, kitty kitty!" Lily called, making her way to the open basement door. "Buttercream?" From the darkness below Lily heard a familiar meow. "Buttercream? Come here, kitty kitty!" She continued to hear the cries. Lily turned back to her sister. "Emily, I think Buttercream is in the basement…*Emily!*"

Emily could not hear her — the music was too loud. Lily turned around and heard the cry again. She sighed and started down the stairs. "Buttercream, mommy's coming," said Lily, trying to sound brave. She slowly walked down the stairs into the basement. Turning on the switch she could hear the faint humming of the lights as they struggled to come to life. Again the cry of her beloved cat came from a far corner of the basement. She slowly walked towards the sound.

Upstairs, Emily had finished washing the dishes. She picked up the dish towel and started to dry them over the sink. She shivered as a cold draft hit the back of her neck and traveled down her spine. Turning to see the basement door open, she walked over to shut it. She shivered

again—the damp basement had made the kitchen

rather cold. She went back to the sink and started

drying a plate. The towel fiber became tangled

around her ring and she pulled it too quickly. The

ring slipped over her knuckle and fell off her hand

into the sink. She tried grabbing it but the ring

bounced around and down into the drain. "Damn

it!" she said, throwing her fists down onto the

sides of the sink. She knew very well her mother

had told her a thousand times to take the ring off

while washing her hands or doing dishes. The ring

was a present from her deceased grandmother and

it was very special to her and her mother.

Turning around, Emily looked over at the

wall across from the sink. There was a switch with

two pieces of masking tape, which in black marker

were labeled "on" and "off." This was the switch

for the disposal. She pressed her lips together,

thinking it through. If she could just get the ring

before her mother found out, it would be like

nothing ever happened. She walked over and

flipped the switch into the "off" position. Going

back to the sink she rolled up her sleeve. First she

lowered her head down into the sink and peered

into the dark hole, but there was no sign of her

ring. Going into the garage, she fished through a

box on the floor and found the flashlight. Walking

back into the kitchen she did not notice the

scarecrow was no longer sitting on the workbench

behind her. She decided there was no going back — this was the only way around the punishment she would face. She pointed the beam of the flashlight down the drain and saw the ring, deep down inside the disposal. She put her hand down the hole and started feeling around.

Upstairs Sam was folding her clothes while Jack played on the floor with his favorite stuffed toy, Mr. Bear, whose face glowed and it hummed nursery rhymes to him. She was in the middle of folding her pants when she heard a faint voice in the distance say, "Honey, can you come down and help me?"

She was surprised to hear Paul back so soon. Walking over to the bedroom doorway, she yelled down the stairs, "I'll be right there!" She picked up Jack as he dropped Mr. Bear. "Daddy's home and he needs mommy," she said as she carried him to his room and put him down on the other side of the baby gate. "Stay right here for a minute and be good. Mommy will be right back." She kissed him on the forehead and he smiled at her. Sam made her way downstairs. Looking around the living room she didn't see anyone. "Paul?" she said as she walked through the dining room toward the kitchen.

When Sam came around the corner she saw Emily with her arm down inside the garbage disposal. She rushed into the kitchen. "Emily! Don't!" she shouted as she grabbed her daughter's arm and pulled it up. Emily's fingertips had just cleared the top of the drain when the disposal roared to life with a loud grinding noise.

"Ahhhh!" Emily screamed as she pulled the headphones off. She could feel the intense vibration the disposal made. Looking at her mother, tears welled up in her eyes.

"Emily what were you thinking?" demanded Sam, tightly holding her daughter's hand.

"I thought it would be ok — I made sure the switch was off…" Emily's words trailed off as she looked at the wall and saw the switch turned to the "on" position.

"You never, *never* stick your hand in the —" Sam's words were interrupted by a blood curdling scream coming from the basement. "Lily?" called Sam. When she opened the basement door and ran down the stairs she could hear the sobbing and fear in Lily's voice. "Lily!" Sam yelled as she searched for her daughter in the dimly lit basement.

"Mommy!" she heard coming from a dark corner. Lily was so scared she had curled up in the corner, waiting to be rescued. Sam threw her arms around Lily and carried her upstairs. She placed Lily on the kitchen counter. "What in the world were you doing in the basement?"

Lily was still sobbing but trying to come out with the words. "Buttercream is down there! He's in the basement and the bad man is going to get him."

"What bad man? Lily, there's no bad man in the basement. That was just a dream mommy had.

Did you hear mommy tell daddy about my dream?"

"But he's down there! I saw him!" protested Lily.

"Buttercream isn't downstairs," said Emily. "I saw him in the garage."

Sam looked down at her daughter's leg, which had a small cut. "Where is your father?" asked Sam.

"Daddy's not home yet," replied Emily as Sam looked at her, squinting in confusion.

"Emily," said Sam, "Go get the first aid kit out of the garage."

Emily ran into the garage and looked through the six vertical shelves that lined the back. She saw the first aid kit, high up on the fourth shelf.

Standing up on her tiptoes, she reached, feeling around with her fingers. She felt something brush her hand and pulled it back. Looking up at the top shelf again, she paused. She saw nothing. Breathing heavily, she shook her head. Again she reached for the first aid kit. It was just out of her reach. "Mom?" she called, looking for some help.

Suddenly the first aid kit came crashing to the ground.

"Emily!" she heard from the kitchen. Startled and confused Emily picked up the pieces of the kit and hurried to the kitchen.

Sam took out some wipes and cleaned the cut. "Lily, please listen carefully, there is nobody in the basement. Mommy just had a bad dream," she said as Lily cowered in disbelief. "Lily, I will show you there is nothing to be afraid of. I will go down and check. Ok?"

"Okay," replied Lily, wiping the tears from her face.

Sam grabbed the flashlight off the counter and headed down the basement stairs. At the bottom she looked around, scanning the darkness. The lights flickered on and off. From the top of the stairs the girls watched her carefully.

"Girls, there is nothing to be afraid of," said Sam.

As the girls watched, she took a step and fell out of sight.

"Mom!" the girls screamed.

"It's ok," said Sam, standing up and wiping her pants off. "I just tripped — that's all." She then heard the sound tiny footsteps scurrying by her. She turned around, slowly scanning with the light. She could see nothing but the junk in the basement. Suddenly a noise startled her — like nails against a wooden board. She quickly scanned back to the old well and the thick round board covering it. Walking slowly towards the well she listened for the sound. Then it came again, scraping at the wood from beneath. "Looks like we have rats in this old well," she said. "Well, at least they can't get in the house."

"Mommy!" cried Lily loudly.

"It's ok," said Sam as she made her way up the creaky basement stairs. "There's nothing to be scared of. Old houses make a lot of noise."

They heard the sound of a car pulling up the driveway and the garage door starting to open.

"Daddy!" cried the girls as they ran toward the garage. At the top of the stairs, Sam breathed a sigh of relief. She closed the door behind her and, leaning up against it, closed her eyes for a moment. She opened them to see Paul as he walked through the door. He smiled at her as she looked at him, biting her bottom lip.

"What did I miss?" asked Paul, looking at Sam's expression, quite pleased that he knew her so well.

"A lot!" replied Sam, breathing deeply again, trying to absorb all that had just happened. Sam had a special gift—she was good at remaining calm under the most pressing of

circumstances. "We need to talk," she said as Paul

came over and kissed her forehead.

"All right, let's go upstairs so I can change

before dinner," replied Paul.

As Sam started walking toward the stairs she

noticed Paul wasn't following behind — he was

heading back to the kitchen. "Sorry — I'll be right

up," he said. "I just need to close the garage door."

Sam nodded and made her way upstairs. Paul

went into the garage. The girls were looking at the

shingles and tools in the back of the car. "Girls,

take Kingston for a walk around the yard before

dinner," he said.

"All right, daddy," replied the girls, putting on

Kingston's leash and leading him out of the car.

Paul opened the passenger door and then opened the glove box. Inside was a small black box. He opened it and walked toward the workbench. The little box contained a small round silver locket. He opened the locket and looked at the tiny pictures. On one side were the two girls, and on the other himself and Jack. Paul smiled with excitement at the perfect gift for Sam. Her birthday was in a couple days and he loved to buy her gifts. It had been a long time since he had been able to afford to get her something special. Now that their lives were changing, he wanted to get her a gift that said, "I love you and everything is going to be all right." Paul placed the locket into the drawer of the workbench and closed it. Quietly he turned, and the scarecrow caught his eye. "Well, Edgar, looks like I did it again,"

Paul said, quite pleased with himself. He picked

up the old scarecrow and examined its gloves.

"Someone must have had serious issues to make

such and ugly thing." He sat Edgar back on the

workbench and covered his head with an old

cloth.

Upstairs, Sam walked down the hall towards

Jack's room. Behind the closed bedroom door she

could hear Jack laughing to himself. She put her

hand against the door and opened it slowly. Jack

was sitting on the floor facing away from her and

looking up at the wall. He laughed again and

raised his hands the way he did when wanting to

be picked up. Slowly he turned around to look at

Sam. Sam stepped over the gate. "What are you doing silly boy?" said Sam, picking him up.

The door suddenly slammed shut behind her. Startled, she turned around. "Just the wind Jack," she said as she kissed his head. "Just the wind."

She jumped again spinning around towards his crib as a nursery chime began to play. "Ha! Aren't we being silly?" she said, walking towards the crib. She could see the light glowing underneath the blanket and she pulled the covers slowly over Mr. Bear. She looked at it perplexed for a moment—she could have sworn Jack dropped it in her room when she picked him up. "How odd," Sam said to herself as she opened the door and stepped over the gate, shutting off the bedroom light. "Must be losing my mind."

She did not see the dark figure slowly cross the bedroom behind her.

Sam walked down the hall and into her room. Paul came up and sat on the bed. Sam went to him, hugging him tightly. "I'm worried about the girls," she said. "Emily almost lost her hand in the garbage disposal and Lily went into the basement by herself."

"Emily put her hand into the garbage disposal?" he asked. "What on earth for?"

"She lost mom's ring—the one she got for Christmas."

"The girls are just going through an adjustment. We moved their whole world and it's going to take them sometime to settle in."

"I know," replied Sam., "but it seems like all these weird things keep happening and I just don't want them to get hurt."

"I'll talk to the girls and everything will be fine," said Paul, smiling at her with appreciation of how amazing she was.

"All right, I'm going to go start dinner," replied Sam as she picked up Jack. "Come down after you change."

"Yes, Mrs. Bolton," Paul replied playfully.

Sam stopped and gave him her "not-in-the-mood" face.

"Ok, I'll be right down," said Paul. "Just don't run the water. I need to get that ring out before we have another incident."

After dinner, Paul decided to have a talk with Emily and Lily.

"Girls," he began, "I need you to understand something. Living out here away from the city can be dangerous. If something were to happen and we needed to go to a hospital, it's almost a half an hour away. I'm not trying to scare you. I just need you to be more careful. Do you understand what I am saying?"

"If we aren't careful, bad things will happen to us," said Emily.

Lily gasped and looked back at Paul.

"I just want you to think things over and ask mommy or me if you're not sure what to do," said Paul.

"Ok, daddy," replied Lily. "I'm sorry,"

"It's ok, girls — give me a hug and go get ready for bed," he said.

The girls ran upstairs. He rubbed his face with his hands. It had been a long day for the family.

That night Emily was fast asleep when Lily rushed into her room.

"Emily....Emily!" said Lily, pulling the covers off her sister.

"What do you want? Go back to bed," said Emily, annoyed.

"Emily, I can hear something in the house."

"It's probably Kingston or Buttercream. Now go back to sleep."

"But I can't. Can I sleep with you?"

Half asleep, Emily scooted over and opened up the covers. She knew that Lily would just keep coming back until she gave in. After shutting

the bedroom door, Lily climbed in bed.

The girls were just starting to fall asleep when

they heard footsteps in the hall. The footsteps

seemed to start at the end of the hall and creep

past their door to the stairs.

"Did you hear that?" whispered Lily.

"Something's in the house! I *told* you so."

Emily got out of bed and opened the bedroom

door. Looking up and down the hall, she saw no

one. Quietly she opened the door to her parent's

room, and they were sound asleep. Perplexed, she

returned to her room.

The noise started again. This time it was

coming from the stairs. It sounded like someone

was walking *down* the stairs. Emily tiptoed back

around the corner and looked down the

stairs. Nobody was there. She listened for a

moment but the old house was silent. She turned

to walk back to her room. The sound came again,

much more loudly now, and started at the bottom

of the stairs quickly coming *up*. With her socks

slipping on the hardwood floor, she ran as fast as

she could back to her room. Without turning

around she made it inside and slammed the door

shut, gasping for air. Lily was sitting up in the

bed, holding the covers tight.

"What was that?" Lily said, pulling the covers

up to her face.

Emily jumped into bed with her sister.

"I don't like it here anymore," said Emily as she

watched the door. The girls listened for a while

but the house was quiet. They both fought to

stay awake but soon they both fell fast asleep.

Chapter Seven

A Long Run of Bad Luck

The next morning while Sam was busy inside the house picking up after the girls, they ran outside to the yard as Paul climbed up his ladder to the roof in preparation for the day's work.

Sam came out of the house, carrying Jack in her arms. "Girls, go ahead and get in the car," she said as she approached the bottom of the ladder. "We have lots to do today. Paul….Paul? I thought you were going to watch Jack while I took the girls shopping."

"I am," he replied. "I have his playpen all set up. He can watch daddy work."

Sam looked over at the playpen set up in the front yard, and then back at Paul. "I'm not sure that's such a good idea. I mean, what if something happens?"

"He'll be fine," he replied. "I'm going to be right up here the whole time. I can see him perfectly. I've got the umbrella set up and he'll be cool in the shade. Don't worry about it. Take the girls and go have fun."

Sam hesitated for a moment as her mind raced with everything that could go wrong. "All right — I just think it's a little weird, that's all," she said as she placed Jack into the playpen with his toys. Sam went into the house and brought Kingston out, putting him on his leash next to the garage. She and the girls got into the car, and then she backed out of the garage, turning around at

the top of the driveway. Heading down to the

road, she looked out her window at Jack in his

playpen. He smiled back at her. She waved at him

as they were pulling out onto the road. Sam was

still worried about Paul's idea to work while

watching Jack. She reminded herself that Paul was

quite capable of taking care of the kids. She

trusted his judgment and tried not to think about

it. "Girls, we have a lot to do today," she said as

she drove down the road to town. "I'm going to

need your help picking up some stuff for the

house."

In the front yard, Paul tied a rope around the

handle of his old wooden toolbox and started

climbing his ladder to the roof. When he reached

the top, he threw the rope around a tree branch above his head. Pulling the rope, he watched as the toolbox began to lift slowly.

From his playpen, Jack watched him intently, fascinated by the toolbox lifting up onto the roof.

Once he had the toolbox, Paul placed it on a small level piece of roof. Taking a moment, he looked down at Jack playing in the playpen. "Hey bud, you my busy man huh?" he said as he started ripping off shingles and letting them slide down to the front of the house. Jack was down below playing with his toys, content with the day's activities.

Paul did not notice a glass pane in the second story window that slowly began to crack. Inch by inch, the crack spread to form a wide web.

Paul worked quickly, every so often looking down at Jack. It was particularly warm that day and after working for a bit Paul began to sweat. He took off his shirt, and standing up to stretch he looked down at Jack. Their eyes met, causing both of them to crack a smile. Then Paul returned to the job of ripping off the old shingles.

Jack looked over at his Jack-in-the-box as the handle began to turn itself slowly, playing its music. Jack began to giggle. The lid popped opened and the clown jumped out.

High overhead, the window broke through.

From behind Paul felt a strong push, shoving him forward. He tried to lean back and catch himself but he over corrected, falling onto his back and sliding down the roof towards the edge.

"Whoahhhh!" he yelled as his boots hit the edge of the gutter, tearing it away from the house. Face first, he hurtled toward the ground. With his eyes pinched shut and his hands covering his face for protection from the impact, suddenly he felt a vise-like squeeze around his right ankle and a massive jerk as his fall stopped. He took a deep breath and opened his eyes, slowly lowering his hands. He was hanging upside down, swinging a little back and forth. The tree above made a creaking noise as it held his weight. Looking up at his leg, he could see that his ankle had become entangled in the rope, holding him suspended. The rope had saved his life. He took another breath and smiled, laughing to himself and celebrating, knowing very well that he had almost just died from being careless.

He spun around to look at Jack, who was standing up in the playpen, staring at his father, in awe of his acrobatics.

"Don't tell your mother," Paul said, smiling at Jack as the baby giggled.

With his fingertips, Paul could just reach the tips of the grass below. No help there. He stretched up, grabbing his pants. He tried to reach the rope but it was just out of reach. He tried again but could only touch the rope with his fingertips, and his back started to ache. The sun was beating down and he could feel its heat. The minutes ticked by as Paul kept giving it his all in short bursts, trying to reach the rope.

Busy trying to free himself, he did not see Jack stand on top of his Jack-in-the-box and then climb out of the playpen. Jack hit the ground and then slowly stood up, using the playpen for support.

Paul was taking a break, looking up at the rope thinking about how best to get undone. He started to feel woozy as the blood rushed to his head. Over by the side of the garage he heard Kingston whine and start barking. He turned to look at him. "I know — quite the predicament," he said to Kingston, thinking the barking was at Paul's expense. "I don't like it anymore than you do." Twisting, he looked at the playpen in the yard. He saw the toys, but no Jack. Perplexed, he looked around; and there was his baby boy,

walking away from him, towards the pond.

"Jack!.....Jack!" he yelled, trying to get Jack's

attention.

Jack stopped and looked at Paul for a moment

before turning around and walking again.

"No, Jack!" Paul shouted furiously, trying to

reach the rope above. "Come here, come to daddy!

Jack!"

Barking wildly, Kingston tugged at the rope.

He knew something was wrong and wanted to go

to Jack, who was walking just beyond his reach.

Upset by the danger, the dog whined and

whimpered.

Jack paused for a moment to look at Kingston,

who pulled hard, trying to reach beyond his rope.

The toolbox above Paul started to slide very slowly, like it was being pushed toward the edge. The weight of the box caused it to tip on an angle and slide down the roof towards Paul. He heard the noise and looked up. "Oh, shit!" he said putting his arms around his head for protection. The tools and the box came crashing to the ground. Everything missed him except his level ruler, which made a small cut on his arm. He looked up to see if anything else was coming down. He knew he had been lucky the heavy hammer or the sharp files hadn't hit him.

Looking back over at Jack, who was almost to the edge of the pond, he yelled out, "Jack! Jack!"

Looking down at the grass, he saw his razor blade. He reached out for it, stretching as hard as he could. The metal just touched the tips of

his fingers and he struggled to reach it. "Come on.

Come on, you bastard!" he muttered as he

stretched his hand. As he swung past it, he picked

it up. He opened the blade, and with all his

strength he grabbed his leg and pulled his upper

body up far enough to reach his ankle. There was

no time for a careful precision cut. He forcefully

dug into the rope. The razor went cleanly through

and cut into his ankle. With a loud snap the rope

gave way and Paul fell heavily to the ground. As

he rolled onto his stomach a sharp pain jolted

through his back. But there was no time to waste.

Jumping to his feet he ran toward Jack. He limped

as he ran tripping over his tools but nothing,

especially his own pain, would keep him from reaching his son.

Jack had toddled to the edge of the pond. He turned and smiled at his father.

"Jack!" shouted Paul as Jack slipped on the embankment and started to slide into the pond. Paul slid to the ground and reached out, and, grabbing Jack's leg, pulled him up and into his arms. Paul sat on the muddy bank of the pond, holding his son and rocking him back and forth. "I'm so sorry, buddy. I'm so sorry." The tears were brought on by fear and the reality that he could have lost his precious son — his baby boy — forever. It would have been his fault. This one moment could have changed his life forever.

When Sam arrived home with the girls,

she parked in the driveway and started walking

toward the garage. In the front yard Paul's tools

were scattered all over the ground. It wasn't like

Paul to leave everything a mess like that. She

stared at them with an increasing feeling of panic.

"Paul? Paul, I'm home!" she called, dropping the

grocery bags and running into the garage toward

the kitchen door. She flung the door open to see

Paul and Jack sitting at the kitchen table. Paul was

holding the rope that had saved his life. Sam

caught her breath and smiled, glad to see they

were both ok.

"What happened?" she asked. "What's with the

rope in your hand and the tools all over the front

yard?"

Paul smiled and looked at Jack. He had decided it was better to tell the truth—not exactly the whole truth, but most of it. "I fell off the roof, but my rope caught me," he said.

"You fell off the roof? Are you okay?"

"I just have a cut and a rope burn, but I'll be fine," replied Paul, lifting his pant leg.

Sam knelt down to look at the burn and the deep cut. Her experience as a nurse made her piece together more than just a fall. "This is a blade cut," she said. "You might need a couple stitches. Why is it a blade cut?"

"Well, I slipped, and the rope caught me. I had to cut it, and it went a little too deep."

"So you were hanging off the roof while Jack was absolutely helpless?" said Sam, looking up at Paul with her angry "I-told-you-so" face.

"He was fine. I got right down and we came into the house." He knew this was a delicate situation, and telling her what really happened would not be the best idea.

Sam looked at him again, questioning in her mind the truth behind his story. She looked up at Jack, feeling thankful that he was ok, and kissed him on the head. "Ok. I'm just glad you're both all right," she said, leaning over to give Paul a kiss. "I'll get the first aid kit. If things keep going on like this, I'm going to need a better one," she said as she walked into the garage.

Paul leaned over to Jack, pressing his finger to his lips. "Shhhhh….Our secret," he said as Jack looked up at him, smiling.

Paul examined the rope. He just couldn't understand how two straight strands of rope had become so knotted around his ankle. Paul wasn't a man of faith, but he had no doubt someone was looking out for him that day.

Chapter Eight

That Bad Feeling

Everyone gathered 'round the dinner table. Paul sat down slowly, his ankle still sore from his earlier acrobatics. Sam started cutting up Jack's chicken as he banged the table with his spoon. Emily and Lily picked at their peas.

Instead of watching the family eat as he always did, Kingston walked over to the basement door. He sat staring at the door, as if curiously listening; then he started barking at it.

"Kingston, no!" said Paul. "Quiet! Go lay down!"

Kingston stopped for a second, turned and looked at Jack, then again started barking at the door.

"Okay that's it! Come on," Paul said, standing up and walking over to the dog. Pulling Kingston's collar, he led him over to the garage door. "Into the garage," said Paul. "We can't have you barking through dinner."

Kingston walked into the garage, turned around, and sat down. He looked at Paul with his sad face. Paul took the box of dog bones off the shelf and tossed one to him. He didn't want Kingston to think he was too mad. As Kingston snatched up his bone, Paul smiled at the satisfied dog. Shutting the garage door, Paul returned to his chair.

"Daddy, why does Kingston have to be in the garage?" asked Lily, not happy that her dog had been removed from the kitchen.

"Well, honey, we can't have him barking through this lovely dinner mommy made, can we?" said Paul, smiling at Sam.

"You're still not even close to off the hook," said Sam, bashing Paul's attempt at forgiveness.

"All right, let's eat," said Paul, trying to change the subject. "Ray invited us over for dinner on Saturday. He's doing away with some of his turkeys and thought we might like to get out of the house."

"What does that mean, daddy?" asked Lily. "'Doing away' with his turkeys?"

"It means he's going to kill them," said Emily.

"Ewwww, daddy," shrieked Lily.

"Emily! That's enough," said Sam in a strict tone, staring at Emily to get her point across. Emily put her head down and played with her peas. "That sounds like a wonderful idea," said Sam sarcastically, knowing full well she would be in for a night of Ray's famous stories.

A loud cry and whimper interrupted her thoughts. The distinct sound of pain came from the garage.

Paul shot up out of his chair and grabbed Emily as she headed for the door. "No, Em! Let me," he said, trying to protect Emily from whatever he was about to find.

Sam lifted Jack from the highchair and handed him to Emily. "Girls, take Jack in the other room while daddy and I handle this," she said

before following Paul into the garage. Paul could

hear a soft whimpering cry behind the car in front

of his work bench. He peeked around the corner to

see Kingston on the ground covered with blood. A

large pair of hedging shears protruded from his

back. Paul knelt down to him as Sam came around

the corner. "Oh, my god, Paul…. What

happened?," said Sam, covering her mouth in

shock. Paul looked at the blood trail leading from

between the shelves.

"He must have bumped into the shelf and they

fell on him," said Paul.

Sam ran into the house and upstairs to grab a

towel. Running back down, she pocketed the car

keys as she hurried past the girls.

"Mom, what's wrong?"asked Emily. "Is Kingston ok?"

"Stay here, girls, and watch your brother," said Sam as she entered the garage. The girls looked at each other with worry at their mom's response. Paul was rubbing Kingston's ears trying to keep him quiet. Sam came around back of him.

"Paul, hold him still—this is going to hurt," said Sam. She put the towel underneath Kingston and then quickly pulled out the shears. Kingston whimpered and whined softly. Sam wrapped towel around his hind end and tied it tightly.

"Let's get him in the car," said Paul. Sam opened the door and helped lift Kingston up and slowly into the car. "I'll be back," said Paul. "Call Dr. Allen tell him we're coming."

Sam nodded and tightened her lips firmly with tears in her eyes. She went over to the wall, pressing the garage door opener. "Don't worry about us," she said. "Just get him there as fast as you can. Call us when you have an update."

Nodding his head in agreement, Paul jumped in the car. As the engine roared to life he reversed out of the garage. Sam watched him go to the end of the steep drive before accelerating onto the road. She could hear the tires screech as he picked up speed.

"Don't worry boy, you're going to be ok. We'll fix you up," said Paul, looking in the rear view mirror at Kingston, who looked back at Paul for comfort. "You *have* to be ok," he whispered, thinking about his family who just wouldn't be the same without him. All Paul could think

about was how fragile his family was at that

moment. He had to do everything he could to save

their beloved family member.

Sam turned and looked at the blood-soaked

floor. She couldn't chance the girls seeing it. She

took a bucket off the workbench and brought it

into the kitchen. Bringing it over to the sink, she

turned on the hot water and reached down under

the cabinet for a sponge. She stood up, and as she

looked out the window she glimpsed what looked

like the reflection of a man with blood on his face

standing behind her. Turning around, she scanned

the kitchen but saw nothing out of the ordinary

except two dark spots on the floor. She slowly

walked to them, peering around the corner into

the dark dining room. She flicked on the light. The room was empty. Returning to the kitchen, she knelt down to touch the dark substance on the floor. They were globs of mud.

"Silly girl, must be losing my mind," she said to herself as she wiped the mud off her hands and returned to the sink. She looked into the window again but there was nothing. Running her hands underneath the faucet, the blood was hard to scrub off but eventually her hands came clean. She didn't know what she had just seen — she couldn't explain it, but it made her start to question her own sanity. Looking over at the open basement door Sam shook her head in disgust. "How many times do I have to shut this door before someone gets hurt?" She closed it and pulled at the handle to make sure it was fastened securely.

"Mommy?" came Lily's voice from the living room.

"Yeah, honey, I'll be right there. Everything is ok. I just need to clean something up." Sam pulled the bucket out of the sink and headed into the garage. She put the bucket down next to the blood, walked over to the wall, and put her finger on the button to close the garage door. Looking out the door to the end of the driveway, she saw a person. In the moonlight it was hard to make out who it was, but the person was definitely looking at her. She stood still, trying not to move. As she stared back, a bad feeling crept over her. What only lasted a moment felt like forever as the figure walked away, disappearing into the trees at

the bottom of the drive. Sam hit the button and,

standing back from the door, grabbed one of

Paul's golf clubs leaning against the wall.

"Mommy?"

Startled, Sam turned around and quickly

pushed Lily back into the house before she could

see the blood.

"Emily!" she yelled as she heard Emily running

through the hall and into the kitchen. "Take Jack

and Lily upstairs into my room. I'll be up in a few

minutes. Lock the door."

"What's wrong?" said Emily.

"Now!" ordered Sam, trying to instill a quick

response.

Emily took Lily's hand and pulled her into the living room to get Jack. Sam went to the front door and locked the bolt before sliding the chain lock on top. Quickly she ran to the back door, locked it, and pulled down the shade. Taking a deep breath, she took the phone off the wall and tapped a number.

"Hello Dr. Allen, it's Sam Bolton. I'm calling because my husband Paul is on his way to your clinic. We had an accident with Kingston. He was cut by a pair of falling hedging shears."

"All right, Mrs. Bolton," said Dr. Allen, "I'll head down to the clinic right now. Don't worry, we'll take good care of Kingston."

"Thank you…he means a lot to us," said Sam, leaning against the basement door. Exhausted, she slid down to the floor.

"I understand," said Dr. Allen as he hung up the phone.

Sam wiped the tears from her face that she could no longer hold back. Her life seemed to be falling apart, and the lack of sleep had taken its toll. She took a deep breath and gathered herself. *Get it together girl. They need you*, she thought as she stood up and went into the garage. She looked out the garage window and scanned the yard. Nothing moved. All she heard were the crickets singing their nightly song. She turned back to the bucket on the floor. Putting on a pair of yellow rubber gloves, she knelt down, and with the sponge she started to scrub.

The bucket of water turned red and the floor was finally clean. Looking at the wet floor, she heard what sounded like faint footsteps behind her. She rose to her feet and looked around the garage. "Buttercream? Here, kitty, kitty," she said, walking around the stacked boxes of home improvement supplies while removing her gloves. One of the boxes fell over and she again heard the sound like little footsteps. She smiled and slowly walked forward. "Buttercream, you naughty kitty, where are you?"

She looked down on the floor. There were bits of straw everywhere. "What have you been eating, you fresh kitty?" she said, kneeling down and picking up some of the straw. She turned around and walked back towards the shelves. "All right, but you're going to be stuck in the garage until daddy gets home." She picked up the shears and dipped the blades into the bucket of water. Then looking up at the top shelf, she wondered, *What else did you put up there?* Turning over another bucket and standing on it, she reached up with her hand and felt around on the top shelf. The bucket wobbled back and forth slightly as she reached as far as she could.

SNAP! Something seemed to viciously bite her hand. She screamed and fell off the bucket to the floor. Grasping the mousetrap, she pulled it off, holding her fingers in pain. "Damn it! Why the hell!" she said, rubbing and shaking her hand, and then looking at it. There was an ugly red

line across the top of her three middle fingers. She

looked up at the shelf and could now see what

looked like a small glove hanging over the edge.

Standing up she grabbed the tip and pulled it

quickly toward her. Down came Edgar crashing to

the floor. She shook her head at how she had

caused herself to be so frightened. "Well, that's

enough for one night," she said, picking up the

scarecrow and tossing it face down onto the

workbench. Picking up the bucket, she headed

into the house, closing the door behind her. She

poured the bucket of water down the sink and

washed it down.

Bringing the bucket back to the garage, she

looked over at the workbench and noticed the

scarecrow sitting up. "Hmmm," she said to herself, not thinking too much about it. She went over and pulled the light cord, plunging the garage into darkness. Closing the door to the garage she stopped hearing a faint giggle. She looked around the garage as the phone rang in the kitchen.

Sam rushed over to answer it. "Hello?"

"It's me, honey," said Paul. "I'm here with Kingston. The doctor gave him thirty stitches. He's going to be just fine."

Sam closed her eyes and breathed a sigh of relief. "That's good news. I'm so glad, and the girls are going to be relieved too."

"The doctor is wrapping him up now. I'll be home in an hour."

"All right, I'll be waiting," said Sam,

hanging up the phone. She didn't want to tell Paul

about the strange visitor or her accident. He had

enough on his plate at the moment. Sam smiled

and laughed — it had been such a long day, and all

she wanted to do was wind down and relax.

She made her way up the stairs and knocked on

her bedroom door. "Girls, it's mommy. Everything

is ok. Come open the door."

Emily opened the door, looking at Sam for

some comforting news. Lily and Jack were

watching cartoons. "Mommy, what happened?"

said Emily, trying to prepare herself for what Sam

might say.

"Is Kingston going to be all right?" said Lily,

turning away from the TV.

"Yes, girls he's going to be just fine. He had an accident and the doctor had to give him some stitches, but daddy will be home soon with him."

"Yeah!" the girls shouted happily as they started to hop around.

"All right, girls," said Sam "Bedtime. Go to your rooms and I'll be in to kiss you good night." The girls hurried to their rooms to put on their pajamas. Sam picked up Jack and took him to his room. "Come on, little man, night time for you too," she said. She laid him on his changing table and opened the drawer.

To her surprise, out jumped Buttercream. He ran from the room. "How long have you been stuck in there, silly boy?" said Sam. Since he was a kitten, Buttercream had been known for his antics. He always seemed to be somewhere he didn't belong.

Sam pulled out Jack's pajamas and got him ready for bed. She laid him in the crib as he blew raspberries at her. "Sleep tight, little boy," she said as she turned on the glowing bear and placed it next to him. Walking out of the room, she closed the door half way before heading to Emily's room. "Goodnight, Em," she said as she kissed her on the forehead and tucked her into bed.

Sam went to close the door. "No! Can you leave it open for tonight?" said Emily.

Sam was taken aback by the request but a lot had happened that night "Ok.... love you," she said.

"Love you too," said Emily, turning over and pulling the covers over her shoulder.

Sam went into Lily's room and sat on her bed. "I want you to try your best to get some sleep," said Sam, knowing Lily would lay awake waiting for Kingston. "Do you think you can do that for me?"

"Yes, I'll try," said Lily as Sam leaned over, kissing her forehead.

Sam went downstairs and into the pantry to retrieve her stashed bottle of wine. She heard the car pull into the driveway and the garage door open. Hurrying into the garage, she was excited to see Paul and Kingston. He hugged her tightly. "I'm so glad you're back," Sam said to him.

"Me too," said Paul. "It was tough, but he pulled through." Sam opened the back seat and Kingston, wrapped in bandages, got up to lick her hands.

"What a good boy you are," said Sam, mushing his face and giving him a kiss on the nose. Kingston hobbled out of the car and they went into the kitchen.

Paul saw the glasses and bottle of wine. "Excellent idea," he said, picking up the bottle and opening the drawer to get the corkscrew.

Sam smiled at him. "It's been so crazy the past couple days, I just want to relax."

Upstairs, Emily was half asleep and her eyes were almost closed. The door to her room creaked open very slowly. She opened her eyes to see a little tuft of hair by her bedside. It moved around the edge. "Jack, is that you?" she muttered. "Go to bed. Mom always lets you stay up too late. Go bother Lily."

The head of hair disappeared. Then from underneath the bed came a loud knocking on the hardwood floor. Thud... thud... thud. Startled, Emily woke up and opened her eyes wide. "Jack, you little brat," she said as she sat up in bed. She leaned out over the bed, looking down and trying to see without falling out. She sat back in her bed holding the covers tightly. A green light glowed from under the bed and chiming music began to play. She jumped out of bed and moved a step away; then, bending down, she saw Mr. Bear glowing green underneath the bed. She got down on her stomach and reached, pulling it closer.

From behind her, she heard small footsteps coming closer. Emily whimpered in fear. She didn't want to turn around. Something inside her froze. Tears started to form as she heard the tap-tap-tap of feet. She swallowed, and slowly turning around she sat up and squeezed Jack's bear tightly.

Edgar was sitting in her desk chair facing her.

Terrified, she started to sob. The door to her room slammed shut, turning the room pitch black. She heard her desk chair fall to the floor, followed by footsteps that ran by her. It took everything she had to try and run for the door. She sprang to her feet and reached for the handle. A strong grip around her ankle pulled her to the floor. Mr. Bear skidded across the room. It again lit up and started to sing. The closet door creaked open behind her. As something dragged her backwards toward the closet she clawed at the hardwood floors and kicked wildly. "Ahhhhhhhh mommy!" she screamed loudly.

The mysterious grip released her ankle. Crawling forward, she again sprang up to grab the door handle. Shaking it, she screamed, "Help me!"

Down in the kitchen Paul and Sam heard the plaintive cries and ran up the stairs. Even the injured Kingston sprang into action, barking as he leaped past them.

In her room, Emily, still fighting to open the door, looked behind her. The floor boards in her closet groaned ferociously and the noise moved towards her.

Kingston made it to the bedroom door first, barking loudly. Then Paul grabbed for the handle wrenched it open. He picked Emily up and started hugging her. A very confused and tired Lily stood in the hallway, awakened by all of the screaming.

"Daddy, he's in there! He's in my room!" Emily cried as Paul turned on the light.

"It's ok, sweetie," said Paul. "Who's in your room?"

Sam stepped in, taking Emily from Paul. "It's okay baby. I think you just had a bad dream," she said.

Kingston went around the room, sniffing the floor, investigating the cause of the commotion.

"There's nobody here," said Paul, looking in the closet.

"I *saw* him," insisted Emily through her tears. "First Jack came into my room. He left Mr. Bear under my bed, and when I went to find it the scarecrow tried to get me!"

"Em, Jack is in his crib," said Sam. "I put him down before you went to sleep. Mr. Bear is with him and the scarecrow is in the garage."

"Honey, I think you had a bad dream," said Paul.

"Em, you can sleep in my room," said Lily, who after hearing Emily's story was looking for any excuse not to have to sleep alone.

"Ok, Em," said Sam, "Why don't you sleep in Lily's room tonight, and Kingston can sleep on the floor with you. He won't let anything bad happen."

Lily walked over to Emily, took her hand and pulled her out of the room. They both went into Lily's room and Kingston followed.

"Paul what's happening here?" whispered Sam with tears running down her cheeks.

"It's going to be ok. Kids have bad dreams sometimes. It's perfectly normal."

"I know, Paul, but did you see her face? She was terrified. I've never seen her look like that before."

"All right, we can talk to them tomorrow. Everything is going to be fine."

Sam started heading back downstairs. Turning around, she looked back up at Paul. "We have to *do* something," she said.

Hearing the seriousness in her voice, he nodded in agreement. He walked down the hall to Jack's room, and as he slowly opened the door something caught behind it slid across the floor. He knelt down and picked up Mr. Bear. It lit up in his hands. Paul carried it over to where Jack was fast asleep. He put the toy down next to him and smiled at his baby boy. Quietly Paul left the

room, closing the door behind him.

Chapter Nine

The Breaking Point

Sam sat up in bed. The room was dark and she looked around and over at Paul, who was fast asleep. The house was quiet. She got out of bed and walked down the hall to the stairs. Tied around the top banister was a rope. She picked it up, wondering why it was there. She heard giggling and saw Jack toddling by the bottom of the stairs.

"Jack?" her voice seemed to echo as she walked down the stairs "Jack?" She went into the kitchen and saw the basement door open. She again heard the giggling.

She slowly started walking down into the basement, and as she did so she heard a voice. It was a soft whisper saying, "He cried out for you." Sam looked around, but there was nothing but darkness.

A beam of light shot forward. She saw Jack standing on the well wall, facing her. He fell back and she ran towards him. Looking over the wall, she could see him falling and falling into nothingness. She jumped forward but was held back by arms tightly wrapped around her. She could see in his right hand a gold ring with the face of a lion. The mane was gold and the lion's face looked silver and it was growling. She screamed for him "*Jack!*" and then she heard a voice whisper in her ear, "It's not real. You can wake up now."

Sam jolted up out of bed, sweating and breathing heavily.

Paul woke up next to her. "What's wrong?" he said as he rubbed her shoulders.

"Nothing, it was just a dream."

"A dream or another nightmare?" asked Paul. He got up and turned the light on. "Looks like everybody is having nightmares tonight."

Sam was at the end of her rope. She hadn't gotten a good night's sleep in a week. "But not the same nightmare every night," she said. "I'm getting so tired of it. Every time I get to the same spot, he holds me back. I need to sleep. My mind is playing tricks on me."

Paul turned off the lights and climbed

back into bed. He pulled Sam close to him and she

placed her head on his chest.

"Try not to worry so much," he said, trying to

get back Sam's positive side. "Listen to the

crickets. There is peace in this place. You'll find

it."

Down the hall, Lily woke up and turned over.

Emily was tucked into bed with her, fast asleep.

Hearing the floorboards creak, Lily sat up.

Kingston got up and walked out of the room

through the open door. He sniffed the ground as

he made his way to the stairs. He stood still for a

moment, and then heard a noise from the kitchen.

He trotted down to investigate. In the kitchen the

pantry door was wide open. He looked inside,

sniffing around. The pantry door slammed shut behind him. The fur on his back stood on end as he angrily snarled and growled at the closed door.

Upstairs, Lily had almost fallen back to sleep when she heard a noise like a whisper saying, "Lily." She woke up, still quite sleepy, to see a black shadow in her doorway. It turned and walked down the hall. "Daddy?" said Lily, getting out of bed and rubbing her eyes. Picking up her stuffed monkey Moogli, she walked out of the room into the hallway. Seeing the bathroom light was on, she made her way down the hall. "Daddy?" She slowly opened the door. There was nobody inside but the sink faucet was turned on and the water was running. She went to the

sink and turned it off.

A noise came from behind her. She looked up

into the mirror to see the closet door behind her

swing open. Spinning around quickly, she backed

up to the sink as far as she could go. She held

Moogli tightly as the attic board in the top of the

closet slowly pulled back. The eyes of the

scarecrow peered down at her. Dropping Moogli,

she ran back into her room and jumped on Emily.

"Emily!" she cried. "Emily! I saw him! I saw him!"

"Saw who?" said Emily, wiping her eyes.

"The scarecrow! He wanted me to go in the

attic, so I ran!"

"Lily, are you sure?"

"Yes! He was in there!"

"I knew it," said Emily, shutting the bedroom door. "Mom and dad think we're making it up. If we keep telling them, they'll just get angry."

"What do we do?"

Emily paused for a moment to think. "We need to catch him and put him in a garbage bag. Then we can walk down the road to the bridge and throw him into the pond."

"What if we can't catch him?" said Lily.

"I have a plan. He never moves around in front of mom and dad."

"All right, but let's do it tomorrow. I'm not looking for him in the dark."

"Agreed," said Emily, extending her little finger to lock the deal with a pinky promise.

The next morning Sam went downstairs to make breakfast. She turned on the stove and opened the pantry. She jumped back and then started laughing. "Kingston, how did you get in there?"

Kingston came running out and went to the back door in the kitchen. Sam opened the door and let him out. The girls came running downstairs and Paul walked down holding Jack. After the eggs and toast were made, everybody sat down. "Girls, I know that lately things have been difficult," said Sam, "and for that we're sorry; but we all need to work together as a family."

"If you girls need to talk about something, we're here for you," said Paul. "Is there anything bothering you?"

The girls glanced at each other and shook their heads. As they started eating again, Paul and Sam looked at each other, knowing very well something had been planned. "All right, girls," said Paul, "if you have something to talk to us about, we're here anytime, no matter what. I just want you to know that."

"Yeah Daddy, we know," said Emily.

"Let's try and have a good day today," said Sam. "Then tomorrow we can go visit Uncle Ray."

After breakfast, the girls went and got dressed and headed outside. They pretended to play in the front yard while loading up their pockets with heavy rocks.

Emily went into the house. Paul was drying the dishes. "Daddy, do you think you could show me the scarecrow?" asked Emily.

"Why do you want to see him? I thought he frightened you."

"I don't want to be frightened of him anymore. I thought maybe if I got to see him, then I wouldn't be scared of him."

"That sounds like a good idea," said Paul. "He's in the garage."

Emily followed her father. Before entering the garage, she looked back through the window of the kitchen door. Lily was outside and Emily gave her a thumbs-up. Lily ran inside the house, went upstairs, and opened the baby gate to Sam's room. Jack was contently playing on the floor while Sam was in the shower. Lily opened the bottom drawers to Sam's dresser and started pulling out all the clothes and tossing them around the room.

In the garage, Paul took Edgar down and placed him sitting up on the workbench. "See Em? He's just an old scarecrow somebody made to scare away the birds. He's really nothing more than a pile of straw and cloth."

"He's not so bad," lied Emily staring into the scarecrow's glass eyes. Trying not to appear frightened, she swallowed hard. Looking up at her father, she smiled. "Thank you for showing him to me. Now I don't need to be afraid anymore."

Lily burst into the garage. "Daddy, Jack's made a mess of mommy's clothes!" she exclaimed breathlessly.

"Great," said Paul sarcastically rubbing his neck. "I'll go clean them up before your mother gets out of the shower." He left the garage to see what kind of mess Jack had created.

Lily went over and took a large black trash bag from the shelf. She handed it to Emily, who was staring at the scarecrow sitting up on the workbench. Emily slowly walked over to the workbench and sprang forward at the scarecrow, throwing the bag over its body. She quickly pulled it off the bench and flipped the bag over. "Now!" said Emily as she opened the bag a tiny bit while Lily pulled rocks from her pockets and dumped them in the bag. Then Emily tied it shut.

"We got him! Now let's get to the pond," said Emily.

Suddenly the bag began to jerk around.

Lily let out a scream as Emily dropped the bag as

it angrily thrashed around. Then Emily took a

deep breath and picked it up again.

"Let's go, Lily," said Emily. She followed Lily

through the kitchen and out the back door.

Dragging the writhing bag, the girls hurried to the

front of the house. They looked into the windows

and saw nobody downstairs.

"Emily, are we going to get in trouble for this?"

said Lily.

"Not if we don't get caught," said Emily." Now

come on."

The girls ran down the steep driveway to the

road. Emily put the garbage bag in front of her

then swung it up over her shoulder. It had

stopped moving. They looked both ways before heading out onto the road. A few minutes later they came to the bridge over the pond.

After finding a sharp stick, Emily put the bag down on the railing of the bridge. "This is for scaring my sister," she said as she repeatedly stabbed the bag with the stick, making small holes in it. The thing inside thrashed violently. Emily angrily shoved the writhing bag off the bridge. "Now it will *drown*," said Emily as they both peered over the railing, watching the bag sink down deeper and deeper into the pond until it disappeared.

"It's done," said Emily.

"It's done," repeated Lily, trying so hard to be like her big sister. They held hands as they walked back to the house.

Sam had the front door open and was calling them. "Lily, Emily….girls!" She shut the door and they watched her walk through into the kitchen and heard the back door open. "Lily! Emily!" their mother called from the back door.

"Come on, let's go," said Emily as she ran with Lily up the driveway to the side of the garage and around to the back door, where they saw their mother.

"Sorry mom, we were playing in the woods," Emily said, knowing her sister would tell the most ridiculous cover story, so she had to spring into action and quickly get Lily in the house.

"Ok, but next time play closer to the house," said Sam. "I called you over and over again. We're leaving in a couple of minutes. I need to go to the grocery store and your dad wants to get some stuff from the hardware store."

"Ok, mom, we'll be right back," said Emily. The girls hurried up the stairs to Emily's room. Emily pulled Lily around the corner and shut the door behind them. "Ok Lil, it's done. We got him and he can't hurt us anymore, but I need you to do me a favor."

"What?" said Lily, slightly annoyed with being dragged all over the house.

"I need you to not tell mom and dad *ever!*" said Emily, giving Lily her most serious face.

"Ok, I won't," said Lily.

"I mean it, Lil. If they ever find out, we're going to be in *big trouble*."

"All right," said Lily.

"Let's go before they think something is up," said Emily, taking her sister's hand and opening the door. The girls went downstairs and into the garage. Emily opened the back door to let Kingston into the car. The girls climbed in and Paul placed Jack into his car seat in the back.

In town, the girls and Jack went into the grocery store with Sam. Paul dropped them off and drove over to the hardware store. He picked out some caulk, PVC pipe joints, and nails, and brought them to the register.

"You've been in here quite often," said the man behind the counter.

"Yeah, I have a big renovation project going on," replied Paul.

"Really? Where you from, if I may be so bold?" asked the man.

"Not far from here. We live in the house next to Hayden Pond."

"Sheriff Bolton's place?"

"Yes, I'm Paul Bolton, Jon Bolton's nephew. Pleased to meet you."

The man paused, taking a moment to look Paul over. "They said the old sheriff went crazy and started spending an awful lot of time up there alone."

"Well, don't always believe what you hear," said Paul, picking up his bags and heading towards the door. "Have a nice day."

"Yeah, you too," the man said, carefully watching as Paul left the store and got into his car.

Paul put his bags in the back seat with Kingston and sat in the driver's seat. Looking into the store window, he could see the man talking to another customer while looking at Paul. It was obvious they were talking about him. Paul smiled back and waved while saying, "What a bunch of small town nuts." The man nodded and Paul drove away towards the grocery store. "Must have nothing better to do then spread rumors," he said to himself as he pulled into the grocery store. He got out of the car to help Sam load the groceries.

"Don't look now, but I think we're the most fascinating thing to happen here since flannel," said Paul as people in the hair salon across

the street gathered at the window to stare at them.

"Remember how I said I wanted to be a movie

star?" said Sam.

"Yeah," replied Paul, looking at the salon.

"Well, I've changed my mind," replied Sam.

"It's not so much fun getting all this attention."

She quickly put the last bag into the car before

ushering the girls into the back seat.

Arriving back at the house, Sam got out of the

car and hurried through the front door. "I need to

go to the bathroom, I'll be right back," she said.

Paul clicked the garage door button above his

head a few times. "Damn thing isn't working. Go

ahead inside, girls. I'll put the car in the garage

after I get Jack a snack." Paul and the girls got out

of the car. Emily picked up a couple of bags

of groceries and went inside while Paul took a

rather grumpy Jack out of his car seat. "Come on,

little man, it's time for your snack," he said. Lily

grabbed a bag and struggled to bring it into the

house. "Emily, can you feed Kingston while I get

Jack a snack?" asked Paul.

"Sure," said Emily, going into the pantry.

Lily, who wanted a job as well, spoke up. "I'll

go get the rest of the groceries."

"Ok, thank you sweetie," Paul said, kissing his

daughter on the forehead. "After you're done,

come in and play with Jack so I can put the car in

the garage." Lily was always eager to help. Emily

went to the back door to bring Kingston inside for

dinner.

Lily walked outside and around the car to the open driver's side door. She hopped into the driver's seat and grabbed the steering wheel. She started turning it left and right. "Here comes Lily in race car number one making her way around the track to the next turn errrrrrrr." Lily was having so much fun pretending she forgot about the groceries.

Thinking she heard a noise from the back of the car, she turned around to investigate. The driver's side door suddenly closed. Lily jumped and pulled the handle but the door was locked. Standing on the seat, she looked around inside the car.

In the house Sam came downstairs. She looked a little pale.

"Sam, can you sit here with Jack?" said Paul. "I want to bring in the car." He picked up his bag from the hardware store and brought it into the garage. Pressing the garage door button on the wall, he opened the bag to make sure he had purchased the correct size nails.

In the car, Lily looked up and saw the garage door opening and her father in the kitchen doorway. He was studying a box of nails as it slipped out of his hands. The nails sounded like chimes as they fell out of the box hitting the cement floor of the garage. Paul bent down to pick them up.

Something caught Lily's eye she looked to the far end of the garage. Sitting on the top shelf facing her was the scarecrow, glistening with wetness. It seemed to be *leering* at her with a sick, twisted smile. Frightened, Lily started to cry. Suddenly the keys in the ignition turned, starting the car. The gearshift lever next to the steering wheel jerked down, into reverse.

Hearing the car turn on, Paul looked up.

"Daddy!" she screamed. "*Daddy!*"

"Lily, no! Hit the brake!" Paul shouted as he tried to run, but stepping on the nails caused him to slip. He placed his hands down, stopping himself from hitting the floor. The car rolled backwards down the driveway, picking up speed as it went. Paul jumped back onto his feet to pursue the car.

Sam appeared at the door to the kitchen.

"Lilly!" she screamed as she ran as fast as she could after the car.

"Lily, hit the brake!" Sam yelled again.

"Turn the wheel!" shouted Paul, running furiously down the hill after her. The car was nearing the bottom of the driveway and headed straight toward the pond.

Lily froze in fear, crying out for her parents. She couldn't move. Everything was happening so fast. She looked at the wheel in front of her as it turned sharply to the right sending the car into a reverse U-turn. The car's momentum drove it backwards onto the lawn, heading uphill towards the house. As the car slowed Paul was able to open the passenger door and jump in. Bending down into the driver's side, he used his hand on the

brake pedal to stop the car. Then he threw the gear

shift into park and turned off the ignition.

Lily, trembling in fear, leaped out of the car

into Sam's arms. She fell to the ground with Lily in

her arms and hugged her tightly. "Lily...Lily,"

Sam cried, holding her tightly. "What happened?

You know you can't play in the car!"

Paul walked over to the driver's side door and

leaned against the car trying to catch his breath

from running down the driveway. Feeling

overwhelmed, he slid down the car and sat on the

ground looking at Sam rocking back and forth

with Lily in her arms. Emily had come out of the

house and stood above them, holding Jack. She

was crying and didn't know what to say.

Paul motioned with his fingers for Emily to come to him. She dropped to her knees holding Jack and Paul pulled them both in and hugged them tightly. Looking up he locked eyes with Sam who was still hugging Lily. She mouthed the words, "Thank you," as Paul nodded his head. The close call had pulled them together.

The girls took Jack back into the house so that Paul and Sam could get the car off the lawn. They sat in the car for a few moments to talk.

"Does anyone else on this planet have worse luck then us?" said Sam, smiling at Paul.

"I'm highly beginning to doubt that, but I still wouldn't change it for the world," replied Paul as he guided the car across the lawn into the garage.

"I don't know what she was thinking. I'm just glad she's all right."

"Me too," said Paul. "Me too."

Inside, the girls were headed upstairs with Jack. "Emily, I *saw* him," said Lily. "I saw Edgar. He's *back*. He's the one who broke the car."

"Are you sure it was him?" asked Emily.

"I saw him when daddy opened the garage," Lily insisted, trying to get her point across. "He was sitting on the shelf. He was all wet. After I saw him, the car started to roll. He was *there*."

"All right, we'll have to think of something," said Emily. "We're not safe as long as he's around. For now, we do everything *together*. Understand?"

"All right," said Lily. "But I'm still scared."

"Don't worry," said Emily. "We'll think of something."

Chapter Ten

Dinner and a Show

Upstairs in the bathroom Sam was getting Jack ready for his bath, while Emily and Lily were in Lily's bedroom trying on their clothes. It was to be an exciting day — the family was going to Uncle Ray's house for a family dinner. It would be the break they needed to get away from the house for a while.

"Emily what are we going to do about *you-know-who*?" asked Lily.

Emily grinned at Lily. She had a plan, and all she needed to do was convince her frightened sister to join her. "We have to *burn* him," she announced confidently. "It's the only way to make sure it's done this time."

"How are we supposed to do that?"

"I don't know yet. I'll figure it out. Don't worry, I'm working on it."

Paul was in the kitchen cleaning up. Today was Sam's birthday, and he wanted to make sure she didn't have to lift a finger. As he walked to the sink he slipped on the floor, whacking his head against the counter. "Ahhhhh!" he rubbed his head, and as he inspected the floor he saw something very curious. There were little muddy spots like small footprints leading from the garage door to the basement door. "What the hell?" he said, touching the mud and rubbing his fingers. He got up and took a roll of paper towels off the counter, which he used to wipe up the mud.

Can't have dirt on the floor on Sam's birthday! After

he had thrown away the towel he paused. *This*

definitely warrants an investigation, he thought as he

opened the basement door. The mud marks

continued down the stairs into the darkness. Paul

went into the garage to grab his flashlight.

Determined to find the source of the footprints, he

proceeded down the basement stairs. At the

bottom he flicked the light switch. It made a

clicking noise but none of the lights lit. There was

a foul smell in the air, like nothing he had ever

smelt before. "Oh my God," he said, holding his

hand over his nose.

Upstairs, Sam felt the warm water in the tub.

She turned the faucet off. "Perfect!" she said to

Jack. "What do you think — time for a nice bath?" As she undressed him, from down the hall she heard a "thud" and the sound of breaking glass. Sam picked up Jack and opened the bathroom door. "What now?....Girls?" she called, heading down the hall to Emily's room.

In the bathroom a handle on the tub began to move. It turned and the faucet started to run.

Sam opened the door to Emily's room. All the pictures she had hung on the wall were on the floor. The posters were ripped up and thrown on the ground. Feathers littered the ground from ripped pillows. It was an incredible mess.

"Emily Ann Bolton!" She yelled down the hall as Lily's door cracked open. "What happened in here? Are you kidding me? Clean it up now!" She angrily turned around and walked back to

the bathroom. Stopping halfway, she turned to

face Emily. "We're going to talk about this later.

I'm serious — you're in a lot of trouble."

Emily walked down the hall to her bedroom,

and as she entered her jaw dropped. She hadn't

even been in her room all afternoon. "You're

going to pay for this," she whispered. "I'm not

afraid of you," she said as she threw a picture

frame across the room. "Lily come look," she

called down the hall.

Lily jumped off her bed and came to Emily's

room. "Oh my gosh! What happened in here?" she

asked.

"Don't you see he's mad at us for trying to drown him in the pond? He did this to get back at me. Of course mom thinks I did it!"

"What if we tell her the truth?" asked Lily.

"No, Lil, we can't. They would never believe us. We would just get in more trouble than we already are. We need to take care of this tonight."

Looking at the mess she nodded in agreement.

Bending down, Sam picked up the clothes from the floor in the hallway. The faucet on the bathtub turned itself again, shutting off the running water. Sam threw the clothes in her bedroom hamper. She went back into the bathroom with Jack. "All right, little man, time to clean up," she said, walking over to the tub with Jack in her arms. Before she could put him in the tub, she heard the phone ring in the bedroom. "Must be Uncle

Ray wanting to know when we're coming over.

We can call him later," she said, kissing Jack on

the head. Jack just giggled.

She started to lower him into the tub. Again the

phone rang. Sighing, she pulled Jack back to her

chest, muttering "Or maybe not" as she walked

back into the bedroom. She picked up the phone

and answered.

"Hello?"

All she heard was the sound of static. "Hello?

Can you hear me?" she said, but there was no one

there.

From the bathroom came a loud bang and a

splash, causing her to drop the phone and hold

Jack tightly. She ran back into the bathroom. Her

four-tiered shelf she used for towels had

fallen into the tub and all the towels were floating

in the water. "You've got to be kidding me," she

said putting Jack down on the floor. Grabbing a

wet floating towel, she felt the stinging burn of the

water and quickly pulled her hand back. Placing

her hand over her mouth she began to cry. She

picked up Jack, hugging him and sobbing as she

fell to her knees.

Lily appeared in the doorway. "Mommy what's

wrong? Why are you crying?"

Sam couldn't talk she was sobbing so hard. *I*

almost burned him. I almost burned my baby. It would

have been all my fault. He would have had go to the

hospital. "I checked the water!" she exclaimed. "I

checked it. It was fine!" She turned and wrapped

Jack up in a towel. "Lily, take Jack into my room. I need to clean up this mess."

Lily, confused but not wanting to question her mother any further, picked up Jack and brought him into her parents' room. In the bathroom, Sam pulled the drain to the tub and put the shelf upright. Her mind was racing. She looked into the mirror. "What's happening here?" she said, trying to wrap her mind around the near-tragedy.

In the basement, Paul was following the muddy footprints. Shining his light around the gloomy cellar he stopped dead when it landed on the well. The thick wooden board that had covered the well was broken in half. Half the board was on the ground and the other half was still across the top. He walked over and shone his light on the board.

He slid aside the board on top. Looking

down into the well, he saw dark water below. All

along sides of the well were long deep marks.

Picking up the other piece of board, he scanned it

with his flashlight. The underneath was covered in

thousands of deeply lined scratches. He put his

fingers on the scratches and ran his hand down,

feeling them.

What kind of rats would do this?

The flashlight fell from his hand and turned off.

With a sigh, Paul put the board down and as he

felt around for the flashlight he heard the sound of

footsteps running by him. He froze to listen. Again

he heard the sound, now behind him. His heart

pounded and his breathing quickened. He felt for

the flashlight and found it. Standing up, he

pressed the button on the flashlight but it didn't illuminate. Taking a step towards the stairs he felt something grab his leg, and as he fell to the dirt floor the flashlight lit up. He scanned the dank basement but saw nothing.

Suddenly Kingston came bounding down the basement stairs, stopped at the bottom, and stood looking at Paul. He started to bark.

"What?" said Paul as he looked at Kingston, but Kingston continued to bark intensely at him. Paul walked over to him. Kingston barked and barked until Paul was only a step away, and then Kingston ran up the stairs. At the top he turned around and barked again.

"What is your problem?" Paul said, climbing the stairs and wiping the dirt off his pants.

Whimpering, Kingston looked back down the basement stairs. Paul shut the door. "Come on, we have to get ready to go," said Paul.

He went upstairs to the master bedroom, where Lily and Jack were playing on the floor.

"Something's wrong with mommy," said Lily.

Paul walked over to the bathroom and pushed the door open. Sam was kneeling on the floor. She looked up at him with tears in her eyes.

"What's wrong?" asked Paul.

"I don't know I just don't know. I don't understand. I checked the water and it was warm so I turned it off. I checked the water — I *know* I did. Then I went to see what the noise was in Emily's room. When I came back I almost put Jack in the tub, but the phone rang."

Paul walked over and helped her to her feet. He hugged her tightly.

"The old shelf with the towels fell into the water. When I picked up one of the towels, the water was *scalding*," sobbed Sam. "I burned my fingers!"

"It's all right," said Paul. "It's ok, Jack is fine. You didn't hurt him. It was just an accident." The words he had lately said much too often resounded in his mind.

"I know, but I almost did something terrible, and I feel like I'm losing my mind," said Sam.

Paul wiped the tears from her eyes. "You're not losing your mind. Things are just really stressful. We have had a run of bad luck and you haven't had a good night's sleep in a long time."

Sam nodded her head.

"How about let's get ready and go have dinner with Ray," said Paul, cracking a smile. "Then when we get home we can put the girls to bed early and relax."

Sam smiled back. Paul was always so good at making her feel better.

"All right, I'm going to go get Jack ready and round up the girls," said Paul, kissing Sam on the forehead. He went into the bedroom and picked up Jack. "Lily, go get ready and leave mommy alone. She needs sometime to herself."

"Ok, daddy," said Lily, running out of the room. Paul stood for a moment looking at Jack. His dreams of living in this beautiful home were becoming a nightmare. At every turn there were dangers. Seeing Sam fall apart over and over was almost more than he could bear.

When the family was all ready to go they climbed into the car. "Can we take Kingston?" said Lilly, worried about leaving him home alone with Edgar on the loose — but of course she wouldn't say that to her dad.

"Um, yeah, I don't see why not," shrugged Paul, opening the back of the car. Kingston took no time to jump in. He loved family rides.

When Paul got into the car he noticed that Sam was quiet and still seemed a little distraught. He placed his hand on her leg. "Ready for some time with your favorite cousin?" he said sarcastically.

"Oh yeah, can't wait," replied Sam, cracking a smile.

"Oh, wait," said Paul. "I'll just be a minute." He exited the car and opened the drawer to his workbench. He wanted to surprise Sam at dinner with her birthday present. He looked thoroughly through the drawer but the little black box was gone.

"Everything ok?" said Sam.

"Yeah, everything is fine—I just misplaced something," replied Paul.

"What?" asked Sam.

"Oh, nothing—just a tool Ray wanted," said Paul casually. As Paul got into the car he ran through his mind what he did with the gift.

Sam stared suspiciously at the old house as they pulled out of the driveway and started down the road. It was all too surreal. She couldn't

shake the feeling that something was terribly

wrong.

Walking along the road, Glenn Stuart and his

mother Ellen waved at the car. Paul slowed to stop

as Sam and Emily rolled down their windows.

Glenn approached the car while Ellen stared at the

girls in the back seat.

"Out for a nice family drive, I see," said Glenn.

"We're going to our cousin's house for an early

dinner," said Sam. She looked over at a rather

perplexed Paul. Remembering they had not met,

she said, "Glenn, this is my husband Paul," rather

embarrassed for forgetting to tell Paul she had met

them.

"Hi, it's nice to meet you," said Glenn reaching into the car past Sam, shaking Paul's hand. "This is my mother Ellen. You'll have to forgive her. She is a woman of few words these days. If you ever need anything don't hesitate to ask."

"Get them away from this place!" hissed Ellen, approaching the car as Glenn grabbed her shoulders. "Take those babies and *leave*."

"That's enough, mom," said Glenn. "Leave them be."

"Why should we leave?" Sam asked, searching for answers herself.

"Because *he* won't ever let you leave," replied Ellen.

"Ok, that's quite enough," said Glenn.

"Don't listen to her — she's having a bad week. Ever since that day she wondered off, all she talks about is your house. She doesn't like change. Don't mind her."

"Don't worry about it. It was nice meeting you," said Paul as he put the car in gear.

"Have fun at your dinner. I'm sure we will see you around," said Glenn waving goodbye.

The car was uncomfortably silent for a few moments when Paul decided to speak up. "Wow, somebody's checked out of the institution early," he said with a grin, looking over at Sam, who was biting her fingernails while thinking intensely about what Ellen had said.

"Just a harmless old woman," said Sam. "She has Alzheimer's."

In the back seat, Emily leaned over to Lily and whispered in her ear, "We've got to be careful."

"Yeah, *real* careful," replied Lily as they stared at each other wide-eyed. Ellen's words, as crazy as they seemed to their parents, made perfect sense to the girls. They knew she was not as crazy as everyone thought. Her warnings were heard loud and clear.

As the car pulled into the driveway, Ray looked up from the engine of his truck. He smiled and waved at them. Paul and Sam smiled and waved back. "Oh boy, here we go," said Sam. Paul laughed and got out of the car. Bursting from the doors, the girls ran up the driveway "Ray!," said

Emily as the girls hugged him. With no children of his own, Ray loved to spoil the girls.

"Girls," said Ray, "Why don't you go inside and ask Debbie for some of those cookies she just baked?"

"Yes!" the girls shouted, running to the door.

With raised eyebrows, Sam gave Ray a look.

"Ummm, just one girls, it's almost time for dinner," called Ray, acknowledging Sam's look and the fact he probably shouldn't have offered cookies before dinner. "How are you, Sam?" he then said, giving her a big hug.

"Pretty good," she replied. "I'd better go make sure they only take one. Come on, Jack." She held Jack's hand as he toddled to the front door.

"Everybody seems happy," said Ray to Paul as they watched Sam and Jack go into the house. Once the front door was shut, Paul turned to Ray.

"Yeah, well, to be honest it's been a rough week," he said.

"How so?" asked Ray.

"It's just seems like bad things keep happening over and over, and there's no end to it. It's making life very hard. Sam hasn't slept right since we moved in."

"Well, there's bound to be an adjustment period with the kids being so young," said Ray reassuringly. "Maybe you just need to give it some time."

"Yeah, and hopefully we'll make it out alive," said Paul jokingly.

"Let's go in and see if dinner's done. You can put Kingston in the pen with Sheldon so they can play." Ray nodded at his beagle jumping up and down in excitement upon seeing Kingston.

"Umm, I'd better not. Kingston is still healing. He had an accident," said Paul as he motioned for Kingston to come forward to show Ray his stitches.

"What happened to him?" said Ray, petting Kingston on the head.

"A pair of hedge clippers fell off a shelf in the garage."

"You are having yourselves a bit of bad luck. He can come in the house. He's such a good boy I'm sure he won't be any trouble."

They turned and, leading Kingston, walked into the house. The smell of turkey filled the air and they both breathed deeply. "Ahhh, is dinner ready?" said Ray, leaning over to give Debbie a kiss.

"Almost. Just finishing setting the table," said Debbie. Sam was laying out silverware while the girls watched TV with Jack.

"Paul, can you grab the highchair from the car, please?" said Sam. "Come on girls, time to eat." The family sat down together at the table. Kingston sat by the girls, just in case they wanted to sneak him some food.

For Sam and Paul, the meal was a much-needed break. They laughed as Ray told stories about when he was a kid. Near the end of dinner Sam decided to do a little digging of her own. "Ray how did you get the house again?" she asked.

"We got a notice of unpaid taxes from the town," he replied, "and I had them look up the records. We thought it was a mistake. Sure enough, dad bought the house thirty-three years ago. He never told us about it. Momma figured it must have been a place he went to relax and have a couple of… sodas," he said, changing his words to reflect the younger audience in the room.

Sam knew all about Jon Bolton's drinking problems. Everyone suspected that's why he had killed himself a couple of years ago. "Do you know anything else about the house?" inquired Sam as she dabbed Jack's mouth with a napkin.

"No, not really. It was nice finding out there was a little something extra. I was happy we could—"

Suddenly a loud noise came from the basement, sending Ray and Paul shooting up from their chairs. "What the hell?" exclaimed Ray as he hustled towards the basement door with Paul following close behind.

They went down to the basement as the girls stood up. "Girls, stay here," said Sam, walking over to the basement door to listen for an update on the situation.

A moment later, Paul came to the bottom of the stairs. "A pipe burst. The basement is flooding. We're going to need to repair it now."

Sam could hear Ray in the background having words about the predicament. Sam was just about to walk away from the door when Ray appeared. "Sam, I'm going to need to repair this. Can you take Henry's plate of food to him?" he said.

"Of course," said Sam. She would much rather take a ride then listen to Ray complain for the next few hours. A family friend of many years, Henry was Jon Bolton's best friend and like a father to Ray. Sam had met him a few times at family gatherings and funerals. Sam started to make up a plate and covered it while Debbie picked up dishes to clear the table.

"Thanks for going," said Debbie to Sam. "Henry lives about fifteen minutes down the main street at a place called Rose Hill Park. You can't miss it. There's a big red and gold sign out front. Just ask the front desk and they will point you in the right direction," she said as she carried the dishes into the kitchen.

"Em," said Sam as she picked up the plate of food and made her way to the door, "You help Debbie with the dishes, and Lily you watch Jack." Kingston followed her out of concern of being left behind. "All right, come on," said Sam, smiling at her excited companion. Sam went outside and opened the back door of the car for Kingston. He jumped in excitedly. She got into the car with the plate of food and shut the door. She paused, taking a deep breath of relief. Maybe it was good thing to have a little time alone with her thoughts.

All the way to the assisted living facility where Henry lived, her mind raced with everything that had happened at the house. She kept thinking about what Ellen had said to her. Something just didn't feel right. She felt uneasy in her own home and the lack of sleep wasn't helping.

Pulling into the half-circle driveway at Rose Hill Park, she parked out front and cracked all four windows for Kingston. Stepping up out of the car, she took a good look at the place. It seemed like a very nice residence. Being a nurse at one time herself, she could appreciate the apparent cleanliness of the facility. The grounds were kept tidy and the abundance of nice flowers made the place very welcoming. She entered and found the front desk, where a nurse was sitting answering the phones.

"Hello can I help you?" said the nurse, who seemed very sweet.

"Yes, I am looking for Henry Parker's room," said Sam.

"Certainly. Mr. Parker is in apartment twenty-three. Here we call them apartments, not rooms. Go down the hall, take the elevator to the second floor, go left, and it's the fourth apartment on the left."

Sam smiled in recognition. "Thank you," she said as she started her way down the hall. Sam marveled at the nice stone floors. She missed being a nurse and all the smiling faces. She made her way to apartment twenty-three and knocked on the door.

"Coming... coming," she heard as the door slowly opened. "Ahhh, hello, how are you?" said Henry. Sam got the feeling that Henry wasn't sure who she was.

"Hi, Henry. It's Sam Bolton, Paul's wife."

"Ahhh yes, yes, of course. Come in come in," said Henry giving her a hug as if trying to make it seem like he had recognized her. "How are you my dear?"

"I'm doing... good," replied Sam. She was always a bad liar.

"Hmmm. Well, come in. Stay a little while. I don't get many visitors anymore," said Henry, removing her coat. Henry had been a

psychiatrist for fifty years and he knew distress

when he heard it. "My dear, sometimes it helps

getting an outside opinion on things. I may be old

but I'm still a good listener. There's not much I

haven't heard and the good thing about telling

and old person is they soon forget."

Sam laughed and smiled at him. "I'm sure

that's not true. You seem as sharp as ever."

"What seems to be the trouble these days?"

asked Henry gently.

"We just moved into a nice house and we were

looking forward to a chance to start fresh. But it

seems like everything is falling apart. My oldest

daughter almost lost her arm, my son could have

been burned, my youngest girl almost hurt in a car

accident, and Paul, he fell from the roof, and if it wasn't for that rope… God knows what could have happened. Even our poor dog almost died."

"I see," said Henry, looking at Sam above his glasses. "That's a terrible run of bad luck. But I also notice something very *fortunate* about these events. You say, 'almost' and 'could have,' which means *didn't*. You might want to look at the more positive side. You must have angels on your side, or you would have told me a very different story, my dear."

"I guess I was focusing so much on the bad I didn't realize how lucky we have been. It's all happened in such a short period of time. Almost more than I can handle."

"I think it's much easier to dwell on the bad then count one's blessings," said Henry. "By looking at the bright side of every conflict, you can obtain a great sense of happiness."

"Maybe you're right. Maybe I just have been looking at everything in a negative way."

"Living life with positivity is living a life worth living."

"Thank you for listening," said Sam. "It's been difficult to say the least. I really haven't slept since the move. I appreciate it, I really do."

"No problem, my dear. It's nice having someone who will listen to an old man. Do you have a long ride home? I don't want to keep you too long."

"No, actually, not at all; we moved very close. It's only about a fifteen-minute drive from here. We live in a house Jon Bolton used to own."

In an instant, Henry's face changed from kindness to concern. "What house Jon used to own?"

"It's a white house over on Hayden Pond."

Henry 's expression grew dark and his eyes narrowed. "Oh, I see," he said.

"See what?"

He shook his head and his mouth turned down. Then, taking a deep breath, he fixed his gaze directly on Sam. "I fear for you and the safety of your family."

"What do you mean?" said Sam, leaning forward in her chair. She reached over to hold

Henry's hand. "Tell me," she said with curiosity and fear.

"I thought I would be able to take this to my grave. It's my fault—I didn't do what needed to be done, but the years passed so quickly. I had all but forgotten about that house." He stood up and walked over to the closet. He opened it and took a box from the top shelf. He turned back to Sam, bringing the box with him. Sitting down again, he carefully wiped the dust off the box. "Sometimes you can forget the past, but it has a way of catching up with you," he said, opening the box and taking out a stack of pictures. He flipped one over so Sam could see. "By the way, Ray knows nothing of this, and I would prefer to keep it that way," he said, peering over his glasses.

"I understand," said Sam. She was willing to do almost anything to know the truth.

"About thirty years ago," began Henry, "Ray's brother, Thomas, a deputy sheriff, was out on an investigation with Brian, his best friend and patrol partner."

"Yes, I know," said Sam. "He was killed instantly in a car crash. I've heard the story from Ray."

"That's what we told Ray and his mother," said Henry with sadness in his voice. "It was easier than the truth about what had happened that night." He took a deep breath and handed Sam the picture. It showed four men standing together with their arms around each other. She recognized Jon and Henry but not the other two. Henry leaned over and said, "This is Thomas and Brian the day they became deputies. We were so proud of them that day. They had been on the force only a year before they were sent to that house on Hayden Pond. I had received a call from Jon to bring my prized bloodhound, Sebastian, to the neighbor's house," said Henry.

"Mrs. Stuart?"

Henry raised his eyebrows. "Yes. The Stuarts have lived there for many years. Jon seemed unusually panicked the night he called me. Little Molly Stuart had gone missing and he needed my help to find her. Jon sent Thomas and Brian to alert all the neighbors. When Thomas didn't check in with the station, Jon headed up to see what was going on. He found Brian with an open wound on his neck, dying in the driveway. When he

entered the house he discovered his own son,

Thomas, hanging by the neck from the banister.

He was too late to help them. Then he heard a

scream coming from the basement. He went down

there and found the homeowner, a man by the

name of Roman Hollick, sitting on the wall of the

old well. He was holding Molly Stuart. He killed

her in front of Jon. Cut her throat and threw her

into the well. Jon was filled with so much rage he

opened fire, killing Roman and sending him down

into that well. After a full investigation it was

found that Hollick had kidnapped and murdered

at least eighteen woman and children *in that house*.

He tortured them before cutting them all up in

some sort of sadistic ritual. He disposed of their

bodies in that well. Later we found photo albums of the victims and a book filled with demonic rituals. We were able to identify all the victims because he took their fingerprints in their own blood and added them to this book. I had the opportunity to examine it. Apparently, in his twisted mind he was trying to use the souls of his victims to leave the door open to the other side. They were to be his steppingstones for all eternity. Of course, at the time I thought the whole thing was hogwash. After we pumped out the well we could only find bits and pieces, nothing to identify a person. We never found the remains of Roman or Molly. The well was built on boulders that led to deep caverns. After a few weeks we stopped looking."

Sam covered her mouth as tears began to run down her cheeks. "That's awful! After all that, why on earth would he want that horrible house?"

"Jon never wanted to go back to the house on Hayden Pond. He never wanted *anyone* to go back to that house, ever again. He promised Mrs. Stuart nobody would ever be allowed to live there. He was a proud sort of man. It shamed him that he didn't know a monster was hiding in his own town. So he purchased the house. He planned to burn it down."

"Why didn't he?"

"After watching so many people close to him die, something changed in him. After losing Thomas he started drinking. He started drinking every day. One day we were sitting in the car—

this was about five days before he died —

and he told me something. Something that *chilled me to the bone*. He told me one night after he had a few drinks he went to the station and filled some gas canisters with fuel. He drove up to that house and planned on burning it to the ground. But after he got out of the car he looked up at the window into the second floor. He said he saw Thomas behind the glass. He then went into the house, and Thomas was there, and they communicated. Jon said he couldn't burn down the house knowing Thomas was there. After that night he went back a few times, and said he and his son would play checkers together. I was not sure if it was the sadness or the drinking that caused his delusions, but I listened nonetheless. He said that he couldn't go up there anymore because there was something else in that house. Not Thomas; it was *something else*, and it wanted him dead. He made me promise if something happened to him that I would burn down the house." Henry paused to wipe away a tear from his eye. "I thought he was in a bad place, so I agreed to do it. After Jon died, I was angry at him. Angry at what he had turned into. So I concentrated my efforts on raising a rather ambitious young Raymond. He needed a father and hadn't had one since Thomas died." Henry looked at Sam with a half-smile. He then took her hands and gazed seriously into her eyes. "Take your children. Get out of that house. Thomas may be there watching out for his family, but there's something else living in that house.

Something evil Roman created. So much death happening in one place is no place for the living."

Sam glanced at the photo. She put her finger on it. "This — I know this. This ring, I have dreamt about it," she said, pointing to the large ring on Thomas's finger.

"Oh, that was a gift from Jon to Thomas when he graduated. Thomas loved lions. They were his favorite animal, so Jon had the ring made to represent the bravery and strength needed for the job with the sheriff's department."

Sam started to cry. "I *knew* something was wrong with that house. Paul is going to be so upset if I ask him to move. I'm not even sure he's going to listen. What if he thinks I'm crazy?"

"Then we do what must be done,"

replied Henry. "What was promised so many

years ago. *We burn it down.*"

"Isn't there any other way?"

"We don't have time to wait. The longer you're

in that house, the worse it will get. There's no

other way. Get your family out of there. I'll come

to the house tomorrow morning while you're gone

and I'll burn it down. I'm sure Raymond has an

insurance policy on it. Things can be replaced.

Loved ones are priceless."

"How would you even get to the house?" said

Sam, trying to reach out for reality.

"Don't worry about that, my dear. I may be old

but I'm still resourceful. I have my ways. I won't

let you down. I'll make it right I promise,"

he said, holding Sam's shoulders.

"We have to, don't we?" said Sam, with tears welling up.

Henry looked into her eyes and slowly shook his head yes.

"All right, we'll do it," said Sam reluctantly. "We have to. Those are my babies."

There didn't seem to be any other way. As for Paul, she didn't think he'd understand because he didn't believe in such things. Sam put on her coat and walked to the door.

"We'll set it right, I promise," said Henry, watching Sam go down the hallway.

She turned back and nodded once. Taking a deep breath, she entered the elevator. After the door closed she held her forehead. "I must be nuts," she said to herself, thinking about the plan.

The drive back to Ray's house seemed to go by quickly as Sam's mind raced with questions and fears for her family. She pulled up in front of Ray's house and sat in the car for a moment. She leaned over and kissed Kingston. "I don't know what else to do. We can always stop him if we want to," she said, looking at her dog. He kissed the side of her face, causing her to smile. She got out of the car and headed into the house.

Everyone was in the living room watching a movie, while Jack played on the floor with Lily.

"Mommy!" Emily and Lily exclaimed, running to give Sam a hug.

"The pipe is all fixed, and we can go whenever you want," said Paul.

"Let's finish the movie," said Sam as she sat next to Paul. Every moment there was a moment spent away from the house on Hayden Pond. A moment where she could think clearly about everything Henry had told her.

Paul would do anything to cheer me up, she thought. She could make a plan for the whole family, even Kingston. A nice drive to the beach would keep them out for the day. Yes, the beach would be nice. In the morning she'd let Buttercream outside. They could leave early and be gone for the whole day. The insurance policy would take care of them until they found a new house. They'd all be safe again.

Chapter Eleven

The Plan

It was a quiet ride home. Sam was in deep thought while the girls whispered to each other in the back. Paul could sense something was wrong. He kept glancing at Sam. She seemed a million miles away.

"What do you want to do tomorrow?" he asked.

"Oh, I thought we might want to take the kids to the beach for my birthday," replied Sam. "They haven't been in a long time."

"Well what do you think girls?" said Paul.

"Yeah that sounds like fun," said Emily.

"Can we get ice cream?" said Lily.

"All right," said Paul, smiling at his girls. He loved his children so much. He was happy that Sam had suggested the trip and that she seemed excited about it.

As the car made its way up the long driveway, Sam stared at their house. The revealed truth made her uneasy. It seemed the house that she had fallen in love with was not a sheltering home for her and the family. It was, now the bane of her existence. The thought of having to spend another night there made her anxious.

They left the car and piled into the house. The girls took Jack upstairs to their room. They needed to talk and knew their parents needed some time alone.

The girls went into Lily's room and shut the door. "Emily, what are we going to do?" asked Lily, hoping her sister had a plan.

"All right, this is the plan," replied Emily. "We need to get him into the garage. Once he's in the garage, we'll shut the door so he can't get back into the house. We need to grab him and put him on the grill, which I'll fill with that stuff dad uses to light it. Then we light a match and hold the cover down until he's gone," said Emily, rather happy with her well thought-out plan.

"That sounds *terrible*," said Lily, shuddering at the thought of burning something up.

"Lily, what else are we going to do? He'll just keep coming back to hurt us or mom and dad. It's our job to make sure we protect them."

Lily stood quietly for a moment. She couldn't help thinking about her mother and father. "Ok....but how are we going to lure him into the garage?" she asked.

"We're going to need some bait," said Emily, raising her eyebrows at her sister.

"You're not serious!" protested Lily. "You want him to come after *me?*"

"I'll be there, too. I would never let anything bad happen to you. We just need him to think you're alone. Can you do it Lily? Can you do it for mom and dad?"

Lily wanted nothing to do with the plan. She thought about how scary it would be just to see him again, but this feeling was balanced by how much she loved her parents.

"What do I have to do?" said Lily, reluctantly.

"Tonight, when everybody else is in bed, we'll sneak downstairs," said Emily, feeling good about planning their revenge. "You can sit in the garage, and if he thinks you're alone he'll come."

"That's all I have to do—just sit in the garage?" said Lily.

"That's all you have to do."

"This better work or I'm telling mom and dad," said Lily in her most threatening voice.

"It will work—I *know* it will," said Emily confidently. "You just have to trust me."

They were interrupted by Paul putting his head into their doorway. "Hey, girls have you seen a little black box downstairs in the garage?"

"No," said Emily looking at Lily.

"No, daddy, I didn't see a box," said Lily.

"Oh, ok, girls. Please let me know if you see it. Go ahead and get ready for bed. I'm going to put a movie on for you in here so mom and I can have some quiet time."

Paul walked past Emily's room, and as he did he heard a load "thud." It sounded like something had fallen. Opening the door, he looked around. A picture had fallen off the wall. He picked it up and hung it back on its nail. There were some feathers still scattered on the floor near the dresser. Taking the small trash can, Paul picked up the feathers. He noticed the bottom drawer to her dresser was open. The drawer was full of feathers. Pulling a handful out, he saw the familiar black box. He opened it, revealing the locket he had purchased for Sam. The locket had scratches dug into its silver case. He opened the locket and was shocked to see the pictures had been scribbled on with black marker, and black dots had been drawn on their eyes. All, that is, except for Emily's image, which was clean. Paul shut the locket and thought for a moment. How could she do such a thing? Emily was not one to act out or do anything this hateful. Paul decided it best to handle it himself. Sam was under enough pressure and this would just be another thing to eat at her.

"Emily?" said Paul loudly.

"Yeah, daddy, I'm coming," said Emily. She walked down the hall and entered the room to see her father looking angry.

"Emily, do you have something you need to tell me?" he said.

Emily stuttered and searched for something to say. Had he found out about her plan?

"Don't bother lying—I found the box in your drawer," said her father.

Emily was so confused she didn't know what to say.

"Your mother is going through a rough time," continued Paul. "She needs us to be strong and supportive. This was supposed to be a gift for her and you ruined it."

"But daddy—!" exclaimed Emily.

"Emily, I don't want to hear it. You have done a very bad thing. This was very hurtful to me and mommy."

"I'm so sorry, daddy," cried Emily,

knowing that telling the truth would only make

him madder. He would never believe her anyway.

Paul stood in silence, thinking for a moment

how to best punish Emily. "I'll have it repaired,"

he said, "but you'll need to help me with chores

until I feel your debt has been paid off." Then Paul

hugged Emily. "Everybody makes mistakes," he

said. "I just hope you learned your lesson. Let's

just keep it between us."

Emily nodded and returned to Lily's room.

"What's wrong?" asked Lily.

"He did it again!" said Emily, angrily clenching

her fists. "He ruined mommy's gift and I'm going

to burn him for it!"

Downstairs, Paul approached Sam while, deep in thought, she was washing some dishes. He put his hands on her shoulders and she jumped away from him. "Oh," she laughed, "You scared me."

"You're awful jumpy," said Paul, massaging her shoulders as she turned around. "Is something wrong? You've been so distant the past couple of days, like the world is against you."

"I've had a lot on my mind and nothing seems to make sense anymore," she said, hugging Paul tightly and wishing she could tell him more. She knew he would probably think she was crazy. It would all be over soon enough. She had to be strong to get her family through the next couple of days. She went over and over the plan in her head.

Henry would set fire to the house and leave. Nobody would notice for a while, and soon it would be done. Sam thought about all the memories in her things she would leave behind. At least she would have her family safe.

Paul kissed her on the forehead. "It will get better I promise," he said. He left the kitchen and went up the stairs. Listening intently, Sam waited to hear the bedroom door open. Then she went over to the pantry and pulled a plastic bin off the top shelf. She opened the top and looked for a file labeled "HOUSE." She pulled out the file and looked through the insurance documents. Upon seeing the words "COVERAGE OF ALL MATERIAL POSSESSIONS UP TO $100,000.00," she breathed a sigh of relief. They would be well covered, and

Ray had his own insurance, so nobody

would be at a total loss. She put the documents

back and placed them on the shelves.

But what if Henry were just a crazy old man?

What if Sam were to hurt her family for nothing?

She wanted *proof*. She wanted to know if the story

was *real*.

There was a way safe to find out.

Sam went into the dining room. Opening the

drawer in the antique chest, she pulled out the old

checkers set. After putting it on the dining room

table, she arranged the checkers on the board, as if

ready to play a game, with the black pieces on her

side and the red ones on the opposite side. She sat

for a few moments studying the board. Waiting

for a sign but the room was quiet. She

sighed with disappointment.

"Sam?" called Paul from upstairs.

Going to the bottom of the stairs, she looked up

to see if her husband was coming down. "I'll be

up in a few minutes," she called in response.

"Ok, no problem," replied Paul. "I'm going to

get the kids ready for bed."

Sam turned back to the board — and what she

saw made the hair on the back of her neck stand

up. The checkers had been *rearranged*. Now they

stood in one single tall stack in the center of the

board. Every other chip was black and every other

chip was red.

She placed her hand over her mouth as a tear

trickled down her cheek. This was what she

wanted and needed — a sign from Thomas that everything Henry had told her and everything she felt was real. Slowly, quietly, Sam entered the room. "Thomas?" she whispered. "Thomas, I know you're here, and I know you've been helping us. I just want to say thank you." Sam looked around the room. "It will all be over soon. I'm taking them somewhere safe."

The floor around the table creaked, and then the bottom drawer built into wall slowly opened. Sam was afraid at first, but then quietly walked over to it. In the drawer was an old envelope. The paper was yellowish in color. She picked it up and opened it. Inside was a ring with the design of a gold and silver lion. It was beautiful and brilliant, and it made her feel good that he wanted her to have it. She put it on her finger and shut the drawer. "Thank you, it's beautiful," she whispered. "It must have made you so happy." Stepping backwards out of the room, she looked around before turning off the light. "Keep them safe," whispered Sam, thinking about her babies. She turned around and made her way upstairs. She felt safer having the ring. It made her feel protected for the first time in weeks.

Sam went into the bedroom to see Paul and smiled at him. "Everybody's in bed," said Paul. From outside the house came a rumble of thunder. "Sounds like a storm is coming," she said. "I don't mind; we could use the rain."

"I think you should go take a shower," said Paul.

Paul followed closely behind her, wrapping his arms around and kissing her neck. He had no intentions of letting her shower alone. She smiled and turned to him. He placed his warm hands around her hips and took off her shirt as they walked into the bathroom. She tossed it onto the floor and he picked her up and shut the door with his foot. He placed her down on the counter and locked the door, making sure they would not be interrupted by the kids. Sam laughed as Paul walked back to her confidently. Paul would be in much better spirits about tomorrow's events if she blocked everything out of her mind and took some time to focus on him. He smiled at her. "You have to be the most beautiful thing I have ever seen," he kissed her chest and she smiled and bit her bottom lip.

He knew just what to say to her and it made her

feel so good. After having three kids and being

together for ten years, knowing he was there for

her made her want him even more.

Downstairs, from the living room Kingston

heard the noise of heavy footsteps coming slowly

up from the basement. As he went to investigate,

the basement door slowly creaked open. Kingston

approached the kitchen and started growling and

snarling. Turning back, he started making his way

back to the stairs, but he couldn't move.

Something was pulling him back into the kitchen.

He fought, but the collar tightened and his nails

scraped along the floor. A drawer opened in the

kitchen and a small extension cord came out. It

slid across the floor closer and closer to him.

As he struggled and whined, the cord flew up and wrapped itself around his muzzle. He couldn't growl or bark to alert his family. He whined, trying to bark. He pulled and shook his head, trying to break free. The force pulled him to the door to the outside, which flew open. He was dragged through the door and outside into the rain. He made every effort to run back inside but it wouldn't let go. The door shut and he whimpered. Outside he ran back and forth but he couldn't bark.

Lightning struck close the house. Through the mud, blood started to bubble up from beneath the ground. As Kingston sniffed at the ground, a string of veins popped up, wrapping around his collar. He tried pulling away, but more and more sprang from the ground around him, tying him down. He could no longer move. He was surrounded by a web of veins that held him prisoner.

Upstairs, Emily slowly opened the door to Lily's bedroom. Lily followed close behind, regretting that she had agreed to such a dangerous plan. They slowly crept down the hall, making sure with every step the boards beneath their feet remained silent. They could hear the shower running and knew this would be a perfect time to sneak downstairs. Emily started down the stairs and Lily followed quietly.

Down in the kitchen, Emily saw the open cellar door and shut it. She then made her way across the kitchen, opening the garage door. "Ok,

Lily," Emily whispered as they went out into the

garage. Emily pulled the barbeque grill out from

in between the shelves. The old grill's rusty

wheels made a horrible screeching noise. Pulling

the nylon cover off was difficult. The fibers stuck

to the top handle, making the grill's metal cover

fly off, crashing to the ground. They both stood

silently, listening for their parents.

"Be more careful — you're going to get us in

trouble," said Lily.

"Ok, ok, I'm sorry," said Emily.

On the shelf near the work bench were two

square metal cans, which she studied. "I don't

know which one it is," she whispered to Lily.

"Just get them both," said Lily. Emily poured a little bit from one can over the charcoal. It looked like some sort of oil. Then she poured some of the other liquid on. This one seemed to be lighter fluid. "That should do it,"said Emily, looking at Lily very seriously. "You know what to do." Emily took the box of matches off the shelf and placed them on the workbench near the grill. She took one out.

"Ready?" said Emily, looking at Lily.

"Ready," replied Lily, trying to convince herself she was brave enough for her terrifying task.

Chapter Twelve

Hell of a Storm

Emily pulled out the red cooler and Lily sat down. Emily went back into the kitchen, leaving the garage door open. At the doorway Emily turned back to Lily and paused for a moment; then she nodded, showing Lily how brave she needed to be.

Lily nodded back and took a deep breath. Emily then quietly opened the pantry door and went in, before slowly closing the door and leaving a crack so she could see.

In the garage Lily took another deep
breath and whispered to herself, "You can do
this." Lily looked up across into the kitchen. "I'm
not afraid of you," she whispered, then waited a
moment listening. Hugging her stuffed monkey
Moogli tightly she spoke louder. "I'm not afraid of
you," her words getting louder the longer she
spoke. "I know you're here and I'm not afraid. I
put you in that bag. I tossed you off that bridge
and I would do it again. If you think you're so
tough, then come get me." She clenched her
monkey tightly. She was scared, but she knew
Emily was close and wouldn't let anything bad
happen to her. She sat there quietly and listened.
The light from the garage barley shown in the
dark kitchen.

Hearing a faint sound, she sat up. It was the creaking of old wood, and it sounded like it was coming from the basement.

The steps sounded small, but each could be heard, starting at the bottom of the basement stairs and ascending to the top. In her hiding place, Emily was trying to be brave but she couldn't help breathing heavily. She covered her mouth with her hand, hiding her location.

Slowly, and with a creaking sound, the basement door opened.

The scarecrow stood in the doorway, not moving, just still as a stone. Frightened, Lily started to cry. The door to the pantry flung open — but Emily did not open it. She stepped back from the door and looked at the scarecrow. Something threw her from the pantry onto the kitchen floor. She looked up at Lily, sitting on the cooler, paralyzed with fear. Emily looked around but she couldn't see the scarecrow anywhere. Looking back at Lily, she tried to get to her feet, but something grabbed her ankle and began pulling her towards the basement.

"Lily!" she cried out for her sister as she fell hard to the ground. She looked back to see what was pulling her but nothing was there. Slowly, then faster and faster, something pulled her towards the basement and the dark stairs.

Lily found the courage to run towards the kitchen door as it slammed shut in her face. She looked through the window to see her sister reaching towards her on the first step before the basement door closed. Then she was gone!

"Emily!" Lily cried, pulling at the door handle, but it was locked. "Emily!" Lily cried again as tears ran down her face. What had they done? The perfect plan had fallen apart and now her sister was gone.

Upstairs Paul and Sam were in the shower he held her against the wall and her arms were wrapped around his neck. She thought for a moment she had heard a noise and paused listening. "Did you hear something?" she asked.

Paul stopped kissing her and listened for a moment. "It's probably just Kingston," he said, continuing to kiss her. The shower curtain was mostly solid blue, except from the neck up it was made of a blue see-through mesh. Paul was facing the wall but Sam could see out into the bathroom. Sam closed her eyes pressing them tightly and lifting her chin. The hot water steamed the room and she breathed it in deeply. When she opened her eyes, standing outside the curtain with his face against the mesh was a man. His complexion was pale white. He stared straight at her.

Sam's body jolted, grabbing onto Paul tightly, almost falling. Paul grabbed her and as he pulled her back to her feet he spun around. "What?" He looked around the bathroom frantically, but not seeing anything he opened the curtain.

"I saw someone," said Sam, beginning to cry. "A strange man was in here," she insisted.

Paul stepped out of the shower and quickly put on his pajama pants. He walked over to the door. The door was unlocked and as he reached for the handle it started to open. He looked back at Sam. She was putting on pajama shorts and a t-shirt. He slowly opened the door and looked up and down the hallway. Stepping out of the bathroom, he carefully listened for the intruder.

Paul looked back at Sam. As she took a step towards the door, suddenly it slammed shut.

From inside the bathroom Sam screamed "No!" as she grabbed the handle and tried to pull it open.

"Sam? Sam, open the door!" Paul yelled, pushing as hard as he could, but the door wouldn't open.

"The kids, Paul! Don't worry about me, go get the kids!" shouted Sam.

Paul threw his shoulder into the door but it didn't budge. He looked down the hallway to see the door to Lily's room creaking open.

"Go, Paul!" he heard Sam shout from the bathroom.

He slowly stepped toward Lily's door, being careful not to make too much noise. Stopping at the doorway of the master bedroom, he looked over at his closet and then looked back at Lily's door. Entering his and Sam's bedroom, he went to his closet and opened the door. Against the wall leaned a baseball bat. He kept it in the

bedroom for this very reason. He quietly grabbed

the bat, not seeing the shadow of the large man in

the bedroom door behind him. It turned and

walked away towards Lily's room. Picking up the

phone next to his bed, Paul tried to call the police

but there was no dial tone. He pushed a couple of

buttons but there was no sound, just static. "What

the hell?" he said, placing the phone back down.

He turned around quickly, thinking he had heard

a noise but there was nothing there. Baseball bat in

hand, he walked back to the door and looked up

and down the hall. Slowly he walked to Lily's

room, listening for any movement. Placing the end

of the bat on the door, he slowly pushed it open.

Peering into the room, he saw nothing out of

place. Reaching for the light switch, he clicked it on and off a few times but it didn't work. He entered Lily's room and whispered "Lily? Emily?"

There was only silence. Outside, thunder boomed, echoing through the house before dying away. The sound of large rain drops on the roof and windows making it difficult to listen for the intruder.

He knelt down to the floor and grasped the blanket Emily used. Pulling it back revealed nothing but a pillow.

Slowly, quietly, he seized the bottom of the comforter of Lily's bed and pulled the covers. To his astonishment, lying in Lily's bed was the scarecrow. As lightning lit up the room, the scarecrow's face seemed to have a devilish grin.

Hearing footsteps, Paul turned back to the hall. "What the heck is going on here?" he said. The silence was broken by a man's slow deep laughter that sent shivers running up his spine. It sounded like it was coming from Emily's room.

From behind him came a series of crashes. He spun back around to see all the pictures on Lily's desk had been knocked to the floor. He looked back at the bed but the scarecrow was gone.

Sam, still a prisoner in the bathroom, took Thomas's ring off the counter where she had left it. Slipping it on, she closed her hand tightly. "Thomas, if you can hear me, please help my babies," she said through her tears. She then went to the bathroom window and tried to open

it, but it too was unmovable.

"Leave them alone!" she yelled.

Gripping the bat tightly, Paul walked out of the

bedroom and down the hall to Jack's room. He

turned the knob but it was locked. He pushed and

pushed trying to force it open, but it was no use—

the door was stuck. Putting his ear against the

door, he listened for any sound. He heard nothing.

The door to Emily's room creaked open. Paul

took his ear away from the door and took a step

towards Emily's room. "Em, is that you?" he

called. He heard a sound like whispers and

giggling coming from Emily's room. "Emily?

Lily?" he said as he walked into Emily's room. He

tried again to turn on the light but the switch only

clicked. He looked around the room, pointing with the bat as he turned. Except for the steady thrum of rain outside, it was quiet.

Buttercream was lying on top of the dresser. Paul approached him and asked, "Where did everybody go?" Buttercream stood up as a flash of lightning lit up the room. The cat looked at Paul and started growling.

"What's wrong with you?" said Paul.

Buttercream hissed loudly at him and hit the floor before running out of the room. The door slammed shut and Paul ran to it, pulling with all his strength. "What the hell is going on here!" he yelled, putting everything he had into opening the door. "Open the damn door!" he shouted.

He heard the floorboards creak behind him. He stopped pulling at the handle and looked up at the back of the door. The room seemed to get colder, and in an instant he could see his breath. He swallowed hard as the creaking of the floorboards behind him made his heart race. He gripped the bat in his right hand and spun around. There was no one. The room was silent.

Without warning the pictures flew off the shelves towards Paul. To stop the glass and frames from hitting his eyes, he put his elbow up in front of his face. The force was so powerful the frames smashed against him, cracking into pieces as they fell to the floor. Dropping the bat, he stepped back against the large wooden armoire.

Everything stopped for a moment.

Lowering his elbow, slowly he opened his eyes.

The closet door opened as if caught by a wind.

He saw what looked like a black shadow of a man

standing in the closet. As the man smiled, Paul

could see his white teeth, and the deep laugh

started again, echoing through his body. The hair

on Paul's arms stood on end.

"Who are you and what the hell do you want?"

he shouted, taking a step forward.

The bat flew up from the ground, hitting Paul

in the back and sending him crashing to the floor.

As he looked up, a harsh whisper came from

the closet: "*All* of them."

The heavy armoire jolted forward and fell on

top of him. He struggled to open his eyes but the

blow to his head caused him to drift away.

There was a deep gash in his leg from the glass. A trickle of blood crept slowly across the floorboards and underneath the door into the hallway.

Downstairs, Lily was trying to find a way out of the garage. She looked around frantically as the lights went out. She stopped, frozen with fear. The lights flickered before coming on and dimly pulsing. She looked back to the door. The light above the doorway shone brightly and pulsed brighter and brighter until it exploded with a loud "pop." The glass shattered and fell to the floor.

Lily screamed, holding her hands over her ears. Paralyzed with fear, she couldn't move.

A man appeared in the doorway of the dark kitchen. In the shadows she could barely see him until he smiled, exposing gleaming white

teeth. Every inch of the man's face was covered by

dark red blood. He tilted his head, looking at her.

Then a pop and flash erupted next to her. Bang!

The grill lit and fire poured from the sides,

blowing the cover off and sending it to the

ground.

Summoning every ounce of strength, Lily ran to

hide behind the car while the flames exploded,

roaring angrily at her. She looked back to the door

but the man was gone. "Mommy!" she cried—and

suddenly the flaming grill started rolling towards

her.

She crawled under the car, and holding her

monkey tightly, she shut her eyes. "Make it stop!

Make it stop! Make it stop!" she said, crying and

shaking. The horn in the car started beeping and Lily started to scream. *"Make it stop!"* she shouted as loud as she could.

Upstairs in the bathroom, Sam heard the car horn. She started pulling at the door handle. "Paul!" she cried, yanking at the door frantically. "Thomas! Help them — help them please!"

The door gave way, sending her across the room onto the floor. She got up and ran out of the bathroom.

Everything stopped all at once as silence fell over the dark house. As Sam was about to run down the stairs she heard a very familiar giggle coming from Jack's room. "Jack?" she said, walking towards the door. Suddenly she slipped on the hardwood floor, sending her backwards down to the ground. Sitting up, she saw a

strange dark liquid all over her back, arms, and

legs. Running her fingers through the liquid it was

thick and sticky. She opened her fingers spreading

them apart. She breathed in deeply and

swallowed. It was blood — a lot of blood — and she

was covered in it.

Chapter Thirteen

A Living Nightmare

Panicked, Sam slipped around, trying to get her footing. Seeing the blood was coming from Emily's room, she turned the knob and opened it a crack. The door stopped — something was blocking it and she couldn't see inside. "Emily?" she said, placing her face against the gap in the door. She blinked once and an eye appeared in the crack. She jumped back against the wall. The eye was no ordinary eye — it was covered in veins with coagulated blood covering the surface.

With her back against the wall, Sam slid on the floor past the room and ran into Jack's room. She shut the door and locked it behind her. A flash of lightning blazed close to the house, followed

by the crack of thunder. As Sam stood against the

door, she could hear her own heart beating loudly

and her tears flowed freely. She looked at the crib

and walked over to it, praying her baby would be

asleep. Breathing heavier and heavier she reached

out to wrap her hand around the bottom of the

comforter. She pulled the covers off, taking her

time to pray he would be there. The glowing bear

lit up brightly in the center of the bed and started

to sing its nursery rhymes.

Her baby was gone.

"No!" Sam cried, pulling everything from the

crib and throwing it on the floor. She started

taking steps back toward the door. She was scared

to leave the room but nothing was going to stop

her from helping her children. All she

wanted was her family out of that horrible house.

"Why are you doing this?" she cried. Taking a

deep breath, she tried to calm herself. Nodding

her head, she readied herself. She turned the

handle and rushed out of the room towards the

stairs. Another flash of lightning filled the house

with light, revealing a black shadow of a man at

the end of the hall.

Sam screamed but the shadow disappeared.

She heard the laugh of her baby boy coming from

dining room downstairs. She looked down the see

a single checker roll out from the dining room to

the bottom of the stairs. It came to a stop on its

side. Sam started down the stairs. She was about

halfway when, hearing a loud noise behind her,

she stopped. She stood quietly, looking

down at the bottom of the stairs. After applying a

small amount of pressure to the next step, she

stopped when she heard a loud creak of the stair

only steps behind her.

She dared not turn around.

Another step sounded behind her. Sam started

shaking as tears ran down her cheeks. Bump

bump… bump bump… the heartbeat of her fear

echoed through the silence. She breathed in but it

sounded like a gasp resonating in her chest. She

felt a cold breath on the back of her neck followed

by a wheezing noise that became louder and

louder. The menacing sound sent a shock through

her body. Her mind resounded with thoughts.

Should I run, should I turn around, should I just stay

still? Feeling another cold breath against her neck she shut her eyes tightly for a second, then opening them she jumped down, skipping a step and running for her life into the dining room. She spun around, throwing a chair behind her. Trying to locate her pursuer, she looked around — but nobody had followed her into the room. "Stop with your games!" she shouted. "Give me back my babies!"

The front door creaked open. She could see the pouring rain outside. This was her chance to leave the house, but she knew she wouldn't. "Stop toying with me — I'm not leaving without them!" she screamed.

The door slammed shut. She could hear a disturbing laugh coming from upstairs. The ghastly sound made her shudder. She had enough of this. Walking over to the bottom of the stairs she looked up. "Come on! Here I am! Take me instead!" she screamed, egging it on.

As if in reply, violent force shoved her backwards, throwing her hard into the wall. As she fell to the floor she struggled to move but lost consciousness.

In the garage, Lily was still underneath the car, clinging to her monkey. Nothing had moved for a while and the garage was quiet. She inched her way to the side of the car and looked up at the kitchen door. The button to the garage door was a little too high, just out of reach. But if she moved the cooler, she could reach it. She wanted to go back into the kitchen and try to save Emily but everything inside her said to run. She took a deep breath. "All right, keep quiet, Moogli, we'll go get help," she said to her monkey. It made her feel better thinking she wasn't totally alone. Tucking Moogli under her arm, she moved out from under the car carefully and quietly. She kept an eye on the grill, which burned with a low flame. Being careful not to make any noise, she put her hands on top of the cooler and pushed it. The garage was filling with black smoke from the burning oil, and she coughed, covering her mouth. The cooler touched the wall and she stopped. Stepping up on the cooler she reached for the button and pushed it.

Bang! The scarecrow jumped into the kitchen door window, sending Lily to the floor. With a scream, she picked up Moogli and ran to the garage door. Slowly, the door started to rise. Behind her she could hear the doorknob to the kitchen door jiggle back and forth, but she didn't dare look back. The garage door suddenly stopped rising — but it had given her just enough space. Dropping to the floor, she squeezed underneath, into the cold soaking rain. She struggled to get to her feet but something grabbed her and pulled back down toward the garage. The garage door motor whined as if something were blocking it, and the strong grasp around her ankle gripped her more tightly. It flipped her over and kept pulling. She reached for the handle at the bottom of the door, holding on tight, screaming and kicking.

She heard the loud crash of the grill falling over and suddenly her ankle was free. Pushing against the door, she slid out. Looking back underneath, she could see the scarecrow. To her amazement, he was on fire and running back into the house.

"Run!" echoed a man's voice from the garage, but she saw no one. The garage door shut with a loud bang, as if it someone had slammed it down. This jolted Lily into action and sent her running down the driveway. The stinging drops of cold rain did not faze her. Running into the woods, she was just happy to be alive. She reached the path, now full of muddy puddles. As lightning flashed, she ran faster. The muddy water splashed against her with every step.

Soon she came to the river. It was full and moving fast below the wooden bridge. She looked back down the path and shut her eyes for a moment. "You can do this," she said to herself. Lily stepped onto the bridge. Slowly inching her way across, she reached the other side. She started to run again. It was raining so heavily the water had nowhere to go. Every step was work, and the puddles deepened as she ran along the old path. Reaching the Stuarts' house, she banged on the door and yelled, "Help! Somebody help us!"

The house lights turned on. Ellen opened the door wearing her robe and pajamas. Lily hugged her tightly.

"What's wrong, child?" said Ellen, kneeling down to her as Glenn appeared from the bedroom.

Lily grabbed Ellen's arms and looked deep into her eyes. "He's got them and he won't let them go," Lily whispered, knowing Ellen would understand.

Nodding in acknowledgment, Ellen hugged her. "It's all right, you're safe now."

"You must be freezing," said Glenn, taking a blanket off the couch and wrapping it around Lily. "It's all right, I'm going the call the police," he said turning to the table to pick up the phone. "Mom, can you grab another blanket?"

There was no response.

"Mom?" he said, turning around. But she was gone. He looked at Lily.

"She said to stay here," said Lily, looking back at the open door.

"Oh no," Glenn said, putting the phone down and walking over to the door. He looked around outside but could see nothing in the pouring rain. "Mom!" he yelled, but there was no answer. He ran back to the phone and called the police as a rumble of thunder shook the house.

"Sheffield Sheriff's Department," said the woman who answered the phone. "What's your emergency?"

"Hello, we need the sheriff up here right away!" said Glenn. "Something is wrong. The little girl from next door came over. She seems real scared, and my mother just took off."

"I understand, sir. Please stay calm. What is your location?"

"Hayden Pond Road. It's the white house on top of the hill — number three."

"Ok, sir," said the dispatcher. "We'll have someone to that location as soon as we can"

"What do you mean as soon as you can?" said Glenn.

"Sir, the storm has caused several accidents and there are wires down all around town. We only have three deputies. One of them will be with you as soon as possible."

"Ok, please hurry," said Glenn, hanging up the phone and turning to Lily. "It's going to be all right. You just need to stay here. I'm going to go help your parents."

"Don't leave! Please don't leave me," said Lily, starting to sob.

Glenn leaned down and hugged her.

"It's ok. Nobody is going to hurt you, I promise. You can stay in my room and lock the door. I'll be right back. I just need to see if everyone's all right."

Although she was tired and scared, Lily nodded in agreement. Glenn took her hand and they walked to his bedroom. She sat on the bed and he went back to the door.

"I'll be right back, I promise," he said. "Keep the door locked and don't let anybody in except me or your parents."

"Ok," said Lily.

Glenn shut the door, went into the hall closet, and put on his raincoat. Walking over to the door, he lifted the hood up over his head. Lightning cracked, lighting up the woods around the house. Shutting the door behind him, he locked it and hurried into the pouring rain.

Lily went over and locked the bedroom door. She got up on the bed and looked the room over. It was not much, but she felt was safe. "Don't worry, Moogli he's going to help" said Lily, hugging her monkey.

Glenn headed to the shed. Looking around at the wall rack, he took down an axe. He made sure the blade was sharp. He wasn't walking into anything unprepared.

Ellen had reached the river. She looked down at the raging water under the log bridge. Taking off her soaking wet robe, she threw it to the ground — the weight was more than she could balance with.

Slowly she crossed the bridge and then stepped off on the other side. After looking back down the path to make sure she was not followed, she sat on the muddy ground, placing her feet onto the end of the logs and her back against a big boulder. She pushed and pushed, shifting the logs of the bridge a few inches until the muddy banks could no longer support them. The logs crashed into the raging river.

Only then did she continue down the path.

In the house, Sam lay on the floor at the base of the staircase. In her mind, as the room spun around her she struggled to stand up at the base of the stairs. Everything around her was silent and confusing. She looked up to see hanging from a rope attached to the banister a body dressed in black and wearing a black hood over its

head. She could hear the loud creaking of the

wooden banister as it supported the swinging

body. She backed into the dining room up against

the table. Hearing a faint giggle, her attention

focused on the kitchen. The cellar door was open.

She ran to the basement door and looked down

into the dark. At the bottom of the stairs, Jack's

bear lit brightly and began to sing a song. She

could hear the giggles of her baby boy.

"Jack? Jack, it's mommy! I'm coming," said Sam

as she headed down the dark staircase. At the

bottom she picked up the bear. The basement

lights flickered on and off. She walked forward,

listening for her baby. The light in front of her

turned on. Thomas stood on the edge of the well. Everything seemed blurry.

"It's time," he said as he fell back into the well.

She heard the sound of Jack crying. Sam ran towards the edge of the well and looked down, but something from behind grabbed her and pulled her back.

Suddenly she jolted awake. Her head was throbbing in pain. She was sore all over. There were bruises on her arms and legs. She blinked, trying to steady her vision. Sitting up next to the staircase, she realized that although what she had seen was a dream, she was still stuck in a very real nightmare. Glancing down at her hand, she noticed Thomas's ring was gone. "No," she cried, crawling around the floor, looking for it. In front of her, below the banister, blood started

seeping up through the floorboards. She pushed

herself back away from it. Getting up, she walked

into the dining room and looked into the kitchen.

"I'm coming," she said, running into the kitchen.

She looked at the basement door. As she reached

for the handle, the door creaked open and she

took a step back. She thought for a moment.

This was his plan all along. He wants me to go into

the basement.

Hesitating, she heard the giggles of her baby

boy. "Jack?" she said, moving forward down the

stairs. Putting her back against the cold cement

wall, step by step she entered the basement. A bolt

of lightning lit up the stairwell just as the door

slammed shut at the top of the stairs. It was now

pitch black. A foul smell hit her nose, causing it to burn. The stench was unbearable and she had to gasp for air through her mouth.

"He cried out for you," a whisper echoed through the basement.

The hair on the back of Sam's neck rose up and the room instantly felt colder. She held her breath in the dark, listening.

When Glenn reached the stream he saw his mother's soaking wet robe lying on the ground. Looking around he called, "Mom? Where are you?" He wanted to cross the river but the log bridge had been washed away. He ran down the riverbank but there was no sign of her. "Damn it!" he shouted. The water was high and moving fast—there was no swimming across. He now had to run all the way down to the road to get to the house. He turned and started to jog along the riverbank.

In the basement, Sam looked around as the lights flickered on and off, glowing dimly. They seemed to have a pulse of their own.

There he was—like he was supposed to be! Jack stood on the edge of the well, looking at her. She was overjoyed to see him but she knew what would happen next. She lunged forward, reaching for him as he fell back into the well.

Reaching the edge, she looked down into the well, but she couldn't see him. It wasn't filled with water but with dark maroon *blood*. She was about to jump after him but something didn't seem right. There was no sound of him hitting the bottom.

"It wasn't real… none of it was real," she said, praying for faith in her own words. "It was just another trick." Standing tall, she shouted to the gloomy basement, "Give me back my son!"

Chapter Fourteen

Welcome Home

As the sound of an angry growl echoed in the basement. The blood deep within the well started to bubble, like boiling water, with tiny bubbles making their way through the thick substance to the surface. Sam was mesmerized by its movement. She could see something coming to the surface. As she watched, a head emerged from the blood, rising up as if being birthed from hell. The head lifted, revealing black eyes and small bits of flesh barely hanging onto his face. He looked up at her and smiled. His white teeth made Sam tremble. His body looked like the skin had been stripped away, revealing the fibrous tissue surrounding his bones. The blood coated every inch except for his bright white teeth.

Looking up at Sam, he laughed deeply. Now he had risen halfway out of the pool of blood that bubbled around him. Sam tried to rise to her feet but suddenly felt stuck. She turned back to see she had been sinking in the mud. As she watched, a tangle of red veins came creeping up through the ground and reached for her ankles. With a scream she pulled at the veins, but they held her tight. Sam looked back down into the well.

"Do you want to know who I am?" growled a raspy voice. The monster's lips did not move but his voice itself resounded from the house and throughout the basement.

"Your Roman...Roman Hollick," said

Sam trembling with fear.

"This is *my* house. Everything in it belongs to

me. Welcome home."

Roman began to laugh raising both his hands as

a spot on either side of him bubbled violently. On

this command, two skeletons emerged from the

bloody pool and began climbing up the sides of

the well. They looked like hundreds of pieces of

bone held together by ropes of veins, creating

human-like skeletons with strands of hair and

small pieces of flesh clinging to their bones. Their

skulls were large and misshapen, and from their

bloody jaws grew great curving teeth.

"No!" Sam cried again, and as she pulled at the

veins they broke and blood pulsed from them. She

rose to her feet and took a step but was

pulled back to the ground. Her hands sank into

the soil, which was filling with blood and turning

to a red mud. As she struggled to return to her

feet, with its sharp nails one of the skeletons dug

into the flesh of her calf and cut her down to the

ankle.

She screamed in pain, digging at the deep mud

floor, trying to get away.

Unhinging its gaping jaw, the skeleton tilted its

head and hissed loudly at her.

Now the second skeleton creature emerged

from the well and began to crawl towards her.

"Mommy?" came a voice from the direction of

the stairs.

Sam whirled around to see Emily standing a few feet in front of her. Her eyes were closed.

"Emily, run!" she cried, but Emily stood still. She opened her eyes. They were full of blood, moving across in dark waves. Small streams of blood poured from the corners of her eyes, down her cheeks, like tears. As if in a daze, Emily picked up a rope off the shelf and slowly walked upstairs.

"What have you done?" Sam said, kicking furiously to free herself. She felt the skeleton climbing on top of her as it made a high-pitched screeching noise. Not knowing what else to do, she screamed as loud as she could, "Thomas! Thomas, help me!"

The house creaked and groaned. The lights pulsed, glowing ferociously. She felt the grip of her captor release. Crawling away quickly, she flipped over onto her back. The skeletons growled and crawled towards her.

Suddenly a heavy support beam fell from the ceiling above the creatures, landing on them and pinning them down as they struggled to reach her.

Then Sam heard a voice pulled straight from her dreams.

"Run!" the voice whispered in her ear.

Sam gasped as Roman's head appeared from the well. He seemed to be supported by the blood at his feet. Sam struggled to her feet and ran up the stairs. The pain of her injured leg made her fall, but her will was strong and she sprang up again. Reaching the top, she kicked the door shut. Taking a kitchen chair, she jammed it against the door handle. Spinning around, she could see the garage was filled with thick smoke.

Ellen had reached the back of the house. She looked through the window and knocked. Sam jumped at the noise and ran to the door. "Ellen? What are you doing here?" she said.

"Listen, child," Ellen replied, gently taking hold of Sam's hand and looking deeply into her eyes. "He won't ever stop till he gets what he wants. Every soul he takes only makes him stronger. Thomas came to me in a dream. He showed me the way."

Sam nodded her head, knowing now that Ellen spoke the truth.

"How do we stop him?" she asked.

"It's all right, dear child," replied Ellen. "I know what I must do."

As they spoke, the creatures clawed and pushed against the basement door.

Cupping Sam's cheeks in her hands, Ellen wiped away her tears. "The only way to send him back is to cut the source of his power," she said. "To free the souls he's using as a bridge to this world."

"What should I do?" asked Sam.

"Get them out of this house and don't ever come back," replied Ellen, kissing Sam on the forehead. "Go, child. I will hold them off as long as I can. Tell Glenn I will always love him."

Sam nodded her head in agreement and, after hugging Ellen, hurried to the dining room to look for Emily.

Upstairs in Emily's room, Paul opened his eyes. The room seemed to be moving around him. He blinked a few times trying to stop the spinning. His head throbbed in pain. The weight of the heavy wooden armoire was difficult to lift. Paul gritted his teeth, feeling a sharp pain in his leg from the glass. He looked down towards his leg. A shard of glass was sticking out. He placed his hands down onto the shattered glass beneath him and groaned as he pushed the heavy armoire up. Using his arms, he inched out from underneath, and then turned onto his back and sat up. He examined the piece of glass and took a deep breath. With a grimace he pulled out the jagged shard. Biting his fist, he leaned forward, moaning in pain. There were clothes all around him. He picked up one of Emily's long-sleeve tops and tied it tightly around his leg to stop the bleeding.

"Emily!" Sam's scream echoed through the house and brought Paul to his feet.

"I'm coming, Sam," said Paul, pulling the door open enough to try and climb through.

From the living room, Sam saw Emily at the top of the stairway.

"Emily!" she shouted. Emily had climbed over the banister and was holding onto the railing with her head tilted to look at her mother. The blood was still flowing around in her eyes and the rope was around her neck.

"We've been waiting for you," she whispered. For an instant her eyes became clear again. "Mommy?" she said, looking into Sam's eyes as she let go and fell from the banister.

"No!" Sam cried, rushing to her and supporting by her feet as she hung from the banister. Choking, Emily tried to pull the rope away from her neck.

"Emily!" Sam cried frantically, trying to hold her daughter up.

"I'm coming!" yelled Paul, kicking the armoire away from the door. Sam heard banging noise upstairs and the sound of footsteps through the hallway.

Paul emerged, covered in blood, and weakly he limped to the banister. Holding his hands together and interlocking his fingers he hammered away at the banister with his fists. It was painful, but Paul didn't care — he would break every bone in his body to save his daughter.

Hearing the screams, Glenn reached the front door of the house but it was locked. "Stay away from the door, I'm coming through!" he shouted as he began to hack away at the door with his axe.

Paul felt a surge of adrenaline as, pounding harder and harder, he heard the wood start to crack. Emily's body went limp as Paul stepped back and, using the bottom of his foot, kicked into the banister as hard as he could. The wood split,

cracking in two as Paul slipped back onto
the floor and Emily fell into her mother's arms.

Sam took the rope from around Emily's neck
but her daughter wasn't breathing. Paul grabbed
the railing, and pulling himself up and along the
banister, limped to the bottom of the stairs. He
knelt down next to them. Sam held Emily's nose,
and tipping her head back she breathed into
Emily's lungs. Paul started chest compressions but
there was no sign of life.

"Come on baby, breathe," said Paul.

Another whack from the axe hit the front door
and Glenn broke through. Through the gaping
hole he saw Paul and Sam trying to revive Emily.
With a final powerful kick the door broke open

and Glenn entered the house and knelt down behind them.

"Emily, come on baby, breathe! Emily! Breathe!" said Paul.

Suddenly Emily started to cough. She opened her eyes and Paul fell back and covered his face. He was crying as Sam picked up her daughter and hugged her. Paul hugged them both and kissed Emily on the head.

"Lily is at my house and she's safe," said Glenn.

Sam looked up and smiled at him. "Thank you."

In the kitchen, Ellen could no longer hold the basement door. It creaked with such force the middle started to bow and the noise of cracking wood filled the kitchen. Blood started pouring out from underneath, causing Ellen to slip.

Having no choice but to allow the skeleton creatures to enter, she stood behind the door as it swung open. As the two skeletons emerged, they looked around the kitchen. Ellen stayed quiet as one of the skeletons crouched on the floor with its grotesque vein-encrusted backbone only inches away. It looked around the kitchen but did not see her behind the door. The sound of voices in the next room drew the creature's attention away from its search. Hissing to alert the other skeleton, they both began crawling across the floor into the dining room.

"What the hell is that?" said Glenn as a skeleton came around the corner.

"We have to get out of here — now!" said Sam. The skeleton bent down low to the ground and pounced, jumping across the room onto Glenn, knocking him to the floor. Sam and Paul struggled to pull the creature off him. Blood bubbled up from the floorboards beneath Glenn. Veins started shooting up through the blood, attaching themselves to the bones of the creature. With great force the veins tightened the skeleton to the floor, imprisoning Glenn.

The other skeleton crawled halfway up the wall before leaping across the room onto Paul's back. He was so weak he could barely fight back, and the skeleton quickly pinned him to the floor.

"Paul!" yelled Sam, trying to pull it off. Sam picked up the axe and approached the creature holding Paul to the floor. She swung it hard, breaking the creature's boney ribs. It writhed and screamed in pain. But a thick vein shot from the floor, wrapping around the axe and pulling it from Sam's hands to the floor.

"Go Sam, run! Save Emily!" said Paul. The veins sprang from the blood pool, wrapping around the skeleton and securing it to the floor on top of Paul. The skeleton pushed its boney face into Paul's, hissing at him. Closing his eyes, Paul turned his head. "Go!" he shouted as the creeping veins covered his mouth, making him unable to speak.

"Emily, go to Lily," said Sam, pushing her out the door. "Run to Glenn's house!"

"Come with me!" cried Emily.

"I'll come when I can," replied Sam. "You run!"

Emily nodded and began to run away from the house.

Sam turned as Roman entered the room. Tilting his head, Roman looked at Sam. The floor and walls of the house groaned and creaked. Roman's lips didn't move but his whispering voice growled from the rooms of the house. "I will bathe in the blood of your children!"

With the words tearing at Sam's heart, she screamed, "You can't have them!"

Roman gave her an evil smile. Lifting his left arm, he closed his hand. Sam felt a pull at her ankle, sending her down to the floor. Roman's hand dropped back by his side and the same mysterious force pulled Sam across the floor to him. "No, no! Let me go! Please!" cried Sam.

"Shhhhhh," said Roman, pressing his finger to his lips. Grasping Sam's ankle with one hand, he slowly ran his other hand along her leg to her thigh. Sam tightly clenched her eyes shut. She could not bear to look at him while he touched her.

Ellen came out from behind the kitchen door. Looking down the hall, she could see Roman's back. Quietly she turned and entered the basement. Following the bloody footprints down the stairs, as she stepped off the last step her feet sank in the red mud. The mud was thick with blood and soil, and every step slowed her down. The lights flickered and went out.

"Molly? Little Molly Stuart, where are you?" she softly called, searching around the basement. She could feel a cold chill in the air. One of the lights blinked a few times and turned on. The blood was pouring slowly from the well like an overflowing tub. "Molly May?" said Ellen. The blood began to bubble again at the surface. Ellen could see something starting to rise up through the blood—first a small skull, and then the little shoulders and arms, clad in a nightgown. As the skeleton rose, the blood started to drip off. Her nightgown and bones became clean and white. Her small porcelain like skull tilted back and forth, looking over Ellen with curiosity.

Ellen walked nearer to her. "My sweet baby girl, I've been waiting for you," she said. A tear ran down her cheek she smiled at the small

skeleton.

The little skeleton walked to Ellen and raised

her bony hand. Ellen took it in hers.

Chapter Fifteen

Go to Hell

The skeleton in the nightgown looked back at the well and pointed with its small boney finger. Ellen nodded and walked with her. Together they stepped into the well. Ellen sank up to her knees in the blood, but then her feet were on something solid enough for her to stand. The blood started to drain back into the well and the level slowly descended.

Ellen looked down at her little girl, who looked up at her. Molly nodded and Ellen smiled. "Don't worry, baby girl," said Ellen. "I'll show you the way. We're going home now." Holding each other's hands, Ellen closed her eyes as they slipped below the surface of the blood. Feeling warmth, Ellen opened her eyes. They were in crystal clear water. Ellen smiled as she looked upon the golden-haired, glowing spirit of her smiling little girl, just as she had remembered her. She could feel warmth of the light guiding them as they slipped deeper and deeper into the well.

Upstairs, Roman stopped as the pool of blood began to drain away from the floor. Sam was shaking. She couldn't stand to look at him. "Leave her alone," said Glenn again, trying to break free from the bonds of the bloody veins. "Take me instead!"

Roman smiled. His deep laugh echoed through the house. Turning toward the kitchen, he dragged Sam along by her ankle towards the basement. Sam screamed and kicked at him, grabbing the molding around the door way as he dragged her through.

"No!" she screamed, slipping along through the blood.

Suddenly Roman screamed in pain as his arm broke away from his shoulder. He looked down at his detached arm with its hand still gripping Sam's leg as she kicked at the ground, backing away from him.

Roman growled as he tried to step toward her — but his legs tore off his feet, which stuck to the ground. He fell to the floor, and with his one arm tried to drag himself closer to Sam.

A high-pitched scream resonated from the house. The blood on the floor started flowing backwards down the basement stairs. Roman and his body parts slid across the floor, flowing together with the blood. The skeletons shrieked terribly as their bones broke away from the floorboards. They dug at the floor as a force pulled them back into the dining room. Their nails scraped the floorboards as they tried to escape the relentless pull. Pushing her feet against the floor, Sam backed away. Desperately, one of the creatures grabbed Sam around the ankle. She was again being pulled.

"Sam, we got you!" shouted Paul as he and Glenn both grabbed her arms.

"Don't let go!" said Sam, pulling her leg free. "Go to hell!" yelled Sam as she kicked the skeleton in its face. The skull fractured apart, shattering into small pieces. The creature let out a piercing scream and clawed viciously at the floorboards as it was dragged back down the stairs. The basement door slammed shut with incredible force.

They were gone.

Sam sat against the wall looking at the basement door. "Thank you," she whispered to herself, knowing whatever Ellen had done had saved them.

Silence again fell upon the house.

Paul and Glenn helped Sam to her feet.

"Where's my mother?" said Glenn, still looking down the hall at the basement door.

Sam shook her head. "She's gone. She saved us," she said as Glenn wiped a tear from his eye.

A noise came from upstairs, breaking the silence. It was a familiar lullaby. Looking around carefully, Glenn picked up his axe and climbed the stairs. Paul and Sam followed close behind him. Together they followed the sound of the lullaby down the hall to the bathroom. Glenn pushed opened the bathroom door with his axe. Looking around, he saw no one. The music had stopped. As Glenn and Paul stepped into the bathroom, something fell from the top of the closet. As it hit the ground it sounded like a small piece of metal.

Glenn picked it up and showed it to Paul. It was a ring with the head of a lion made of gold and silver.

Sam looked up into the open attic hatch as her smiling baby boy appeared. "Jack?" said Sam as she climbed up the shelves.

Jack giggled with delight to see his mother. Sam reached up and brought him down, hugging him tightly. Paul hugged them both.

Together again they went downstairs. The place was a disaster there was mud and splintered wood pieces everywhere.

Hearing a familiar bark, Sam turned to the front door. "Kingston?" she called. A soaking wet Kingston bounded in from outside. He barked, excited to see the family.

As Sam kissed his head she looked outside through the broken door. The sky was turning pink, welcoming the sun.

Suddenly the whole house seemed to groan, and the noise of boards breaking started upstairs and moved towards them.

"Let's get out of here," said Glenn.

As they hurried out the front door they saw smoke billowing from the garage. The noise of the sirens grew louder as a police car pulled into the driveway.

Paul held the ring in his hand looking it over. Sam took the ring from him and kissed it. Closing her eyes, she said, "Thank you, Thomas. We couldn't have done it without you." She knew none of them would have survived that night without Thomas, and she was thankful he kept her baby boy safe.

The officer picked up her radio. "We have a Fire at 3 Hayden Pond Road. All available units please respond."

"Tell them to take their time," said Paul to the rather perplexed officer.

The flames quickly engulfed the roof of the house, and Sam knew there was no saving it. She smiled in relief — they had survived and the nightmare was over.

The officer pointed to something over behind the garage. "Is he yours?" she said.

Sam walked over and picked up Buttercream. "Yes he's ours," she said, hugging him. Sam was overcome with the feeling of gratitude to have every member of her family safe. Watching

flames consume the house brought them peace.

A cab pulled into the driveway and up to the

house. Henry emerged and walked over to the

family. He looked over them, covered in dry blood

and looking like they had come through a war.

"So it's done is it?" he said to Sam as they watched

the flames. She nodded, trying to grasp the terrible

events of that night.

"It's done," she replied. They stood for a

moment in silence. "I'm going to go get the girls,"

said Sam, walking away from the house. Carrying

Jack, Paul turned and limped along behind her.

As Henry stood looking at the burning house,

he had the odd sensation that someone was

staring at him. He looked into the woods but saw

nothing. Turning back to the driveway he started walking to the cab.

From deep in the woods, Edgar — blackened by soot and singed — peered out from behind a tree looking at the house before disappearing into the forest.

Henry opened the door to his cab and looked back at the house. "Well, old friend, you can rest now, it's done." He nodded and climbed back into the cab. He felt warm in his heart. He knew no one would ever go back to that house on Hayden Pond.